AF392075

AN EXPENDABLE SOUL

LIFE AND LOVE IN SIBERIAN EXILE

by Maria Rodziewiczówna
and Tom Pinch

Maria Rodziewiczowna, aged about 27, or about the
time this book first appeared in print.

A few necessary words

1. Maria Rodziewiczówna

Maria Rodziewiczówna (1864-1944) was an extraordinary person in many different ways.

She was born a daughter of Polish gentry in what is today Belarus. Belarus, a country and a nation of its own and independent today, had been for many centuries a constituent part of the Grand Duchy of Lithuania and, as such, a member of the Polish Commonwealth—a multiethnic, federal constitutional republic with an elected king as its "president for life" (as we would say today) and far-ranging civil and personal liberties. Yet, in 1795, that Polish Commonwealth collapsed, and Maria's "Grand Duchy" came under the direct and autocratic rule of Moscow.

Her birth made Maria's self-identity complex: she was a Russian subject, but she felt loyalty to her Polish ethnicity and her Catholic religion, both suppressed and persecuted under Russian rule. And she also felt a sense of loyalty to another community, too: a community of "Lithuanians"—former citizens of the Grand Duchy of Lithuania, that political entity from a better and more liberal past: her neighbors, and co-residents of her part of the world, who may have been ethnic Poles, or Lithuanian-speaking Catholics, or Belorussian-speaking Orthodox, or shtetl Jews. And all of them felt oppressed and exploited by the official Russian party line that a Russian subject had to speak Russian and attend the Russian Orthodox church and submit unquestioningly to the tsar, and everyone who did not was a recalcitrant resister and had to be corrected.

In the wake of the January Uprising (1863-1865) in which all her "Grand-Duchy" neighbors rose against the Russian rule; and which was eventually crushed by Russian troops with extraordinary brutality, her family, like hundreds of thousands of others, was stripped of their property and their legal status as gentry and exiled to Siberia. "An Expendable Soul" describes what Maria saw and learned during that exile.

Returning to Poland after the general amnesty of 1871, her family lived in very difficult economic circumstances until they inherited a large, indebted, and mismanaged estate in Belarus. Since her father died at about the same time, it fell to the 18-year of Maria to take over the management of the property. To be taken seriously by her staff, she cut her hair short and donned man's clothing—and she never took it off again.

She turned out to be an excellent property manager. In the next 30 years, she paid off all the estate debts, improved productivity, drained marshes, built roads, mills, distilleries, and schools, and introduced modern methods of farming.

She never married but lived in a long-term relationship with two other women. The nature of this relationship was never revealed but was widely suspected as being "unorthodox."

During this time, she also wrote novels: forty-six in all. Written in brisk but beautiful prose, they remain highly readable today, and nearly all are still in print. A few, like *A Summer of the Forest Folk* and *An Expendable Soul,* are considered modern classics.

2. "Internal exile"

An Expandable Soul tells the story of internal exiles in Russia about the year 1870. What was internal exile?

Like ancient Assyria and Babylon, Russia has practiced large-scale ethnic cleansing for centuries. (And it still does in Ukraine today). Called "internal exile" or "resettlement," it was different from "katorga" (forced labor) in that the persons subjected to this "administrative measure" were not enslaved but only assigned a new place of residence: a province, or even a county where they were supposed to settle and which they were not allowed to leave for a certain period of time (often 25 years). This was enforced by an elaborate scheme of internal passports and visas. (Internal passports are controlled right on the first page of the novel).

Russian officials felt that the program killed two birds with one stone: 1) removed political trouble-makers from their natural milieu (such as Polish political activists from Russian-occupied Poland) and placed them in a new setting where they could not count on ready support if they meant to continue their opposition activities; and 2) helped populate empty parts of the empire where no Europan wanted to move. Between nostalgia for home and adjustment difficulties, the internal exiles often did poorly, but some adjusted well, and some, being the only people with technical or scientific qualifications in their new milieu, thrived.

An Expendable Soul shows us a portrait of the Polish exile community in the Tobolsk province, in Western Siberia, about the year 1870. We see their different ways of coping, their failures and successes, embedded in a beautifully written and moving portrait of the awesome nature of Siberia (like the great *burun* blizzard) and various fascinating aspects of its life (such as the great winter fair of Kurhan).

I enjoyed immensely working on this translation mainly because of these moving descriptions of Siberian realities.

3. Why a new translation?

This book appeared for the first time in English translation in 1900. That translation suffered from a few problems: first, its British diction sounds somewhat archaic to modern ears; second, it leaves out many important passages of the original Polish; third, it contains a few mistakes; and fourth, it is unclear in several places. I preserved as much of the 1900 translation as I could, but probably more than 50% of the new translation is mine. For the shortcomings of that 50%, I alone am responsible.

Tom Pinch
The Ardennes National Park
Luxembourg

AN EXPENDABLE SOUL

TABLE OF CONTENTS

CHAPTER I
Thirty Below

THIRTY below did not feel very painful owing to the absence of all wind. It seemed that the currents of air were frozen, and on the white ocean of snow, no movement could be seen nor the slightest whisper heard.

The government road leading across this vast space, and marked at every verst[1] by a post, shone like a mirror; here and there on the horizon, some small bush could be made out, but nowhere a larger tree, nor any trace of men; it was light because of the snow, but neither moon nor stars showed in the heavens: it seemed as though their rays were also frozen.

A man walked alone along this endless road. He was warmly clad and walked briskly; he still had some warmth in him, gained at the last post-station, where he had stopped before nightfall.

The official there had looked at his passport, found it in order, and asked where he wished to go.

"To the village of Lebiazha."

"It is not on the government road, but all the same, I can give you post-horses."

"How far is this village?"

---

[1] *Verst*: a Russian measure of distance, about 1km or 0.7 miles

"About forty versts."

"Is there any other village on the way?"

"Yes, about ten versts from here, there is Petrofka. Do you wish for horses?"

The traveler blushed, hesitated, and then answered:

"No, thank you; I will go on foot."

It was very strange. But a man who possessed a legal passport and traveled without police escort was entitled to his peculiarities, so the official did not insist but merely said:

"You had better have something to eat—have some tea."

The traveler consented. In such cold and at night, it was better to walk with an empty pocket than to ride with an empty stomach. So he had something to eat and paid for it. After that, there remained only twenty kopeks in his pocketbook. Then he went forward boldly.

After a while, the red light of the post-house became smaller, then it disappeared. The traveler walked softly in his felt boots, and only the sound of his stick on the hardened snow was heard from time to time. At first, he neither felt light-hearted, nor was he afraid of anything; he was warm and joyful. There were no posts to indicate the versts, but it seemed to him that ten versts was a small distance, and he would see the village at any moment. He had passed so many hundreds, indeed, thousands of versts; what were ten more? But he quickened his step as he perceived something gray in the distance; on approaching, however, it turned out to be nothing but bushes, and disappointed, he slackened his pace again.

Through constantly looking at the snow, and because of the cold, his eyes slowly filled with tears and burned as if with fire; when he closed his eyelids, they immediately froze; he rubbed them with his rough glove and then noticed that his fingers had become stiff. His neck itched from the heavy tulub, and the snow creaked beneath the soles of his boots. Then he slipped and fell. At that moment, his overcoat accidentally opened, and the cold air struck his chest. He wrapped himself up immediately and beat his sides with his hands, but the warmth had gone forever.

Again and again, he trembled and shivered; he began to run in order to warm up but soon tired.

He stopped for a while and looked behind him. Should he turn around? The instinct of self-preservation drew him in that direction; but ambition and desperate energy urged him forward. He gathered his forces together, leaned forward, and went on.

Fear and weakness seized him; he began to hum with blue lips, but it seemed to him that with the air, he swallowed pieces of ice, and he ceased. Finally, he walked like a machine; he thought of wolves, of highway robbers, of death. One of these alternatives would befall him, but which? Perhaps all three by turns: robbers would take his clothes, the cold his life, the wolves his body. He now walked slowly and became sleepy. It seemed to him that he had walked not ten but a hundred versts; perhaps he had lost his way? The road was hardly visible. He lost all strength and courage.

He stopped, looking around with eyes half-asleep, and whispered to himself,

"It was my destiny to come here and stop. I shall never return alive among the living. I am lost."

Once again, he looked for some object on the steppe—for some hope, but could perceive nothing. Then he sat down on the ground and abandoned himself to his fate. And as he sat there resigned to slowly dying, the dead emptiness was broken by some sound; it was the ringing of horse bells, and he was delighted to hear it. He sprang from the ground; perhaps they rang only in his ears?

No, it was salvation: there were lights, too. He could already hear the hard stamping of the horses, and for him, the bells rang the moment of his resurrection. He cried with a hoarse voice and ran towards the noise, fearing to be passed by. But the black shape on the snow stopped, and someone answered his call. Everything grew black before his eyes, and unearthly joy overwhelmed him.

A troika[2] came towards him, reached him, and stopped.

"Who are you? Why do you shout?" asked the coachman.

"For Heaven's sake, help me!" he said, afraid he would be refused. "How far is it from here to Petrofka?"

"Three versts; we are going there."

"Take me then. I will give you twenty kopeks."

"Madam," the coachman turned to his passenger, "let him sit with us. Even if he be a murderer, he will not be able to overcome us both."

The woman passenger said:

"Sit down beside me; are not your hands or feet frostbitten?"

"I don't know. It seemed to me I was dying."

"Such cold as this is trifling," growled the coachman. "You must be a stranger."

"Yes, I come from Europe."[3]

"Aha! Well, sit down. It's none of our business."

The man was about to sit down when a threatening bark resounded from the sleigh.

"There is a dog," said the traveler. "Will he not bite me?"

"Well, it's not his fault if you are a thief or a murderer," said the coachman indifferently. "He wouldn't bite a good man."

At this, the man slipped his hand into the sleigh and touched the dog, which raised its head, smelt his hand, and stopped barking. The stranger sat quietly.

"Well, don't be angry that I suspected you," said the coachman, whipping the horses. "The dog barked before he

---

[2] A carriage or a sleigh pulled by three horses

[3] By what he meant "The European part of Russia"; in fact, the traveler is coming from Poland, then occupied by Russia.

8

smelled you."

They rushed along like the wind. Neither of the two travelers spoke a word; consequently, the traveler remained silent also. The dog lay at his feet, its green eyes gleaming in the dark. Suddenly the red lights of houses shone forth; they came to a stop before an inn.

"Here is Petrofka; where would you like to stop?" asked the lady.

The traveler alighted and stumbled. He opened his overcoat, pulled out his purse, and handed her his last money.

"I thank you for having saved my life," he said, ashamed of the smallness of the amount.

The coachman burst out laughing, and the lady shrugged her shoulders.

"Keep your money. I am satisfied with your thanks."

Then she turned to the coachman and said, in a voice accustomed to command:

"I shall·be ready in half an hour, have the horses waiting but do cover them up against the cold."

She then alighted, and her enormous yellow dog jumped out behind her. She entered the inn.

The traveler followed her into the warm saloon. A few peasants sitting there glanced at him and greeted the woman.

"I greet you, Marya Kazimierovna."

"How are you?" she answered kindly.

From a backroom, the innkeeper appeared.

She stretched out her hand to him, and he kissed it respectfully. The innkeeper's wife and children then entered, and all surrounded the woman as though she were an old acquaintance. The inn became animated.

The traveler sat down at a table and asked a peasant,

"How far is it from here to Lebiazha?"

"About twenty versts."

"How much do they charge for a sleigh to go there?"

"One rouble."

The traveler dropped his head.

"Where are you going?" asked the peasant in turn.

"To Lebiazha."

"Aha! To settle there?"

"I don't know."

"Have you been sent here for resettlement?"[4]

"No." He pulled out his passport quickly and showed it, but the peasants were not curious.

"How far have you come?" they asked him.

"From Europe. I have already been traveling for three weeks."

"Marya Kazimierovna," said one of the peasants, "this man is heading to your village."

At that moment, the traveler looked at the lady who had saved his life. Having removed her furs, she sat opposite the innkeeper with a book and a pile of money before her. Evidently, she was going over the accounts. She was young and sad; her eyes seemed tired from tears; her lips were closely shut as though from great grief; her face was troubled but full of dignity. She slowly raised her head and looked at the stranger. She now observed him for the first time. He had dark hair and a broad, undistinguished face, which was, however, beautified by youth, and a pair of dark eyes with a straightforward and honest look in them. He was tall, well-built, healthy, and strong.

Their glances met; he, looking as though ashamed of his misery and need, she, looking indifferently at him. She did not answer but continued her accounts. Meanwhile, her coachman brought a large barrel and a well-filled bag into the room. The innkeeper's wife took these from him and carried them into the backroom. The coachman sat down beside the stranger, drinking a glass of tea that had been given him. They began to talk, and the stranger treated him to vodka but drank nothing

---

[4] Internal exile, a common form of punishment in Russia for political prisoners.

himself.

"You are going to Lebiazha. Perhaps we shall meet you there," he said.

"Most likely. A village is not the world. To whom are you going?"

"To Doctor Gostinski."

"Well, no doubt we shall meet then. He is my master, and here is his daughter!"

"Miss!" he called out to her, "we have plucked our visitor from the snow."

This time the woman looked at him with more interest, and the traveler rose.

"I beg your pardon," he said, timidly as ever. "Has your brother mentioned my name to you?"

"You are Antony Mrozovetski?"

"Yes, madam."

"My brother spoke of you and was waiting for you," she answered sadly, her lips scarcely pronouncing the words. "But he is no longer with us."

She turned her head aside and struggled for a moment with her emotion.

"He died two weeks ago," she added with an effort.

The traveler did not say a word. He turned toward the window, great tears dropping from his eyes. The inn became as silent as a tomb. Apparently, the woman did her sums, but she did not see the figures, and neither did she remember where she was. From the window, the sobbing of the stranger was heard.

At length, the innkeeper said:

"God's will! Do not cry, Miss."

And the coachman blew his nose noisily, adding:

"Death should take thieves. Why did it take him?"

The peasants shook their hands, and one of them said:

"It would have been better if it had taken the old man, not the young. But no one can help that, can they."

The traveler did not change his position. Turned to the

dark window, he complained to the night, weeping quietly, forgetting even his own dreadful situation in the presence of this last blow. Someone spoke to him, but he did not comprehend it and did not answer. Only when he felt a hand on his shoulder did he shudder and turn around.

The young woman stood before him, wrapped in her furs, ready to go. She was quite calm now.

"Let us be going," she said simply, as though it had been obvious.

He obeyed silently.

He sat beside her in the sleigh, and they took off at a gallop.

"A month since I had a letter from your brother," he said timidly.

"A few days later, he took a cold, followed by inflammation of the lungs, which he was too weak to withstand. Everything happened with surprising rapidity. Oh, this winter! This winter! One must become accustomed to it. He was very delicate."

"How is your father?"

"He bears it," she answered gloomily. "How long is it since you left the country?"

"Three weeks."

"I have been here five years already—ever since my mother died. Father has been here twenty years."

"I am afraid I shall only remind him of his grief. It will, perhaps, be better if I do not go to your house and you do not mention me to your father."

"We are not accustomed to dissimulate. We have been waiting for you, and we shall see you gladly. Antony loved you."

"Thank you."

"Here we are, home already," said the coach- man.

Indeed, the sleigh was already running down a village street which was very dark and empty. They stopped before a fence that separated a very comfortable, two-storied house from the street. There was a light in the house, and when the woman opened the gate, two large dogs rushed joyfully toward her. The door of the house opened, and a man with a lantern appeared; he was homely and thin and showed his decayed teeth as he laughed.

"Good evening, Sergey. Open the stable gate for Grinya," she said, taking the lantern from him.

They entered the hall, from which stairs led to the upper story.

Someone opened a door downstairs, from whence came warmth and the smell of the kitchen, and on the threshold appeared an old woman, a bonnet on her head.

"Is that you, Marya?"

"Yes, aunt."

"Thank God. I was uneasy already. I will serve supper immediately."

"Is Father alone?"

"Father Ubish was with him, but I think he has gone."

In the first room upstairs, the young woman took off her furs, as did Mrozovetski. He remained only in his leather vest and felt shoes, much ashamed of such clothing and the lack of any valise. He trembled from fatigue and hunger.

"Come with me, please," said the young woman.

In the second room, warmed by a fire in the fireplace, sat old Doctor Gostinski. He stretched his hands toward his daughter, smiling sadly.

"No untoward adventures along the way?"

"No, father. I bring a guest with me, Mr. Mrozovetski."

The old man rose quickly. He was still strong and healthy, but his hair was snow-white. He approached the young man, looked at him, and without a word, pressed him to his heart. They understood each other in that silence.

"Where did you meet my daughter?" asked the old man after a while.

Mrozovetski blushed.

"I must tell you at once," he said. "In Tobolsk, I had a very unpleasant accident. Being very tired, I entered the first inn I came to in order to rest for a couple of days, and the first day they stole my trunk and my money."

"You must thank God they did not kill you."

"They did not; and they even left me fifteen roubles. I went by post as far as the money would take me and then, forty versts from here, I started to travel on foot."

"A crazy notion!"

"I overestimated my strength and should have died along the way had I not met your daughter."

The girl was no longer in the room.

"Well, you had a narrow escape. No frostbite on hands or face?"

"No, I am alright."

"And how do you find Siberia?"

"It is dreadful!" answered Mrozovetski frankly.

"Oh, and what would you call it if we had a snowstorm to welcome you?"

He spoke softly and rapidly as though afraid the stranger would ask about his son; he realized that he must tell him eventually but had not sufficient strength. The newcomer, however, did not ask about his son.

They were not left long alone. A woman—the same he had seen downstairs—came into the room.

"You come from Europe?" she asked impetuously, her eyes shining.

"From Vilnius."

"My God! My God! I am sure you had knelt in Ostra Brama."[5]

"The day of my departure."

---

[5] The Gate of Dawn is a city gate in Vilnius, the capital of Lithuania, and one of its most important religious, historical and cultural monuments. It is a major site of Catholic pilgrimage in Lithuania.

"Then you saw the vicar there? He is my own brother."

"Yes, I saw him, and had I known of the relationship, I would have paid him a visit."

"Don't think he is their relation," she said, pointing to the host. "Not at all, only mine. I am a stranger here; I belong to another family. My maiden name was Szeygwillo; and I married an Utovich. The vicar Szeygwillo is my brother. He must be old—it is twenty years since I came here with my husband! He must be grey?"

"The man I saw during mass had dark hair."

"Is it possible? Well, it is possible; in our family, one does not become grey very soon. My hair is white; but it's on account of the climate."

She shook her head and became thoughtful for a while, assured about her brother's dark hair. Then she said:

"He must be in good health, although he hasn't written to me for five years. Antony promised me to inquire about him, but he forgot it, poor thing."

When the dead man's name was mentioned, Mrozovetski looked timidly at the old man and shivered, for his gaze was returned. Again they understood each other in that mute glance, and the father was relieved. He would not be obliged to tell of his grief.

The old woman roused herself.

"Here I am talking and forgetting to tell you that your supper is ready. Grinya has told me about your misadventure. Come and eat. Marya will be with us shortly, she only went down to the store to fetch something."

Mrozovetski understood from this that she was the housekeeper, and when she disappeared behind the door, the doctor, taking advantage of her absence, said:

"Her brother is not in Ostra Brama. He is in the cemetery. But no need to talk about it to her—she has had enough other grief! She is a widow and an orphan. For ten years, she has lived with us. Her husband and her two children died here."

They entered the dining-room. Miss Marya appeared, and all sat at the table. Mrozovetski could not eat for fatigue. Mrs. Utovich asked him a hundred questions, and in the meanwhile, Miss Marya told her father about her journey.

"In Krynka, I got seventy roubles, and in Petrofka fifty-three. Somebody must go to- morrow to Kurhan to get some vodka. I think I shall go myself, as I need many things for the store."

"Perhaps it would be better to send Grinya with a letter to Shumski. He will run the errand."

"Always in the worst way. I prefer to do it myself."

"As you like. Have you prepared the room for our guest?"

"Will he stay with us?"

"Why not? We have an empty room."

The girl said nothing. She had risen, and Mrozovetski could hear her giving some orders to Sergey. After a while, the women retired. The doctor pointed out to the newcomer the door of a room and said gloomily,

"This room is empty now. You will be comfortable there. You must excuse me for not accompanying you, but I have not been inside it for two weeks."

Having said this, he turned swiftly-away.

The empty room was comfortably furnished, large, and warm. The floor was covered with a carpet, and on the walls were suspended arms, skins, stuffed birds, some Kirgiz costumes, their monstrous idols, and many other such things.

One could see it had been occupied by a student—one with higher education and a curious disposition. The bookcase was filled with books and doctors' instruments.

But Mrozovetski had no strength even to think of his dead friend. He fell asleep and slept like a log

CHAPTER II
You Shall Remain Here Forever

SERGEY, in his cook's dress, stood beside the sleeping man. He was attended by a white cat, who also looked with curiosity at the bed.

Mrozovetski awoke and sprang up, startled by the clear daylight. Evidently, he had overslept.

"What time is it?" he asked.

"No matter what time it is. You have slept forty-eight hours," answered the cook, smiling.

"Impossible!" exclaimed the young man, dressing hastily.

"Why impossible? When I am sick, I can sleep thirty-six hours. Is it not so, Katalay?" he asked the cat. "The old woman sent me here to ask if you were not sick. What an idea! A young man sick!"

"Are all at home?" asked Mrozovetski.

"The old man went to visit his patients; the young girl went to the city on some errands; and the old woman sits in the store. It's always that way. The priest sits in the kitchen because it is cold everywhere else. When the young man was living, he traveled, but he is no more. Well, Katalay, let us go and look after our cutlets."

He went towards the door, the cat after him.

"Did you notice how intelligent he is?"

"Who?"

"My Katalay. He could be a priest to these Sibiraks."[6]

"Are you not one of them?"

"Thank God, no! I am from Europe. I was a cook in a restaurant in Moscow. Now I'm unhappy. Well, Katalay, jump!"

He stretched his foot out towards the cat, who jumped over it, then they went out.

Mrozovetski dressed and then stood at the window. Through it, he could see the courtyard and the barn, with, further on, an orchard; and, beyond that, the interminable steppe.

The young man thought over his position. He had come to a friend who had invited him to come. In Europe, he had lacked work and bread.

"Here, if only one can raise a little capital, all business is easy."

So the dead man, his good and true friend, had written. By hard work, he had saved some money and had come. He was now at the end of his journey, but without money and without friends. What should he do? Pray for a while on his friend's tomb, and then return? But how? He had only fifteen kopeks, and all the clothing he possessed was on his back.

What should he do? What should he do? He thought, unable to move further, unable to find a logical way out of a humiliating situation. Must he then beg from strangers?

"How do you do?" sounded Mrs. Utovich's voice from the dining-room.

Awakened from his reverie, he rubbed his eyes and forehead and came out to greet her.

"You are rested, thank the Lord! Come to the kitchen,

------

[6] The Russian population of Siberia

please, and have your breakfast, there it's warmer."

They went to a large room where Sergey and Katalay were housekeeping. At the table sat an old priest, drinking tea. Mrozovetski saluted him, and Utovich performed the introduction.

"This is Father Ubish, our boarder, and this is Mr. Mrozovetski, who, a month ago, was in *Ostra Brama*, and saw my brother, the vicar."

"I have been to Ostra Brama," answered the priest indifferently.

"But when? A hundred years ago!" said the old woman.

"No matter! If I want to go, I will go there anytime," retorted the priest testily.

The old woman pointed to her forehead and then whispered:

"He is a little confused. No wonder—this climate!"

While serving breakfast to Mrozovetski, she said:

"Then you knew our Antony? He was a good boy, and that's the reason he didn't live long. Poor Doctor—he brought him up and now has nothing. Now he cannot forgive himself for bringing the boy to this climate. But it's always thus—when God gives you one thing, He takes another away. Fortune smiled on him. Oh, he is rich! He owns this house and plenty of land, and cows and horses. In business, too, he is lucky. During the summer, he trades in cattle, and in the winter, in grain. Money flows into his coffers from everywhere. Even the store pays him well, and from the dram shops he has a good income, too. Well, all this good luck turned around to be Antony's misfortune. When the old doctor's wife died, I advised him to bring Marya here. She was in Vilna, at a boarding school then. So Antony brought her here, then went back to those studies of his. When he finished his university in St. Petersburg and became a doctor, the father set his head on getting him here. So much work, he needed help. True enough! And then it was his vocation--medicine. Well, everything turned out badly. Poor thing! He did not help his father long—he didn't manage much work; but the long grief remains, and many tears have flowed here."

"He received the Sacrament!" added Father Ubish quietly, nodding his head as though he would say: "He has no more sorrow; he is better off thus."

"It's easy for you to say that. You didn't have any children of your own," brusquely answered Mrs. Utovich.

"How do you mean, I didn't?" said the old priest. "I had my parish," he added and became gloomy at once.

"Now I pray every day for Marya. She is healthy but delicate, and she must do her brother's work. Ah! These riches, these riches. They cause such sorrow! I don't know how it will end, for you must know she is engaged to Shumski, who directs Shishkin's vodka distillery. He must stay here three years, and after that, he will probably go back to Europe and take her with him. What then shall we two do with the good doctor?"

She grew thoughtful, but at this moment, two peasants entered, asking for sulfur and tobacco.

"Come and see our store," she called to Mrozovetski.

The store was situated behind the kitchen. It contained everything: sugar, tea, cotton, ropes, leather, biscuits, and an endless variety of other things.

The peasants purchased some sulfur, and while going out, they munched it as if it were candy.[7] After them came some young girls who asked for thread, soap, and face powder. Looking at their rough and pock-marked faces, Mrozovetski could not help smiling.

"Yes, they powder and rouge their faces," affirmed the old woman, "and think it looks very natural."

"Or maybe just –better?"

Mrozovetski remained in the store, watching the various

----

[7] The local diet being low in sulfur, made the raw mineral an essential snack

types of Siberians. In general, they were well-built people with honest, open faces. They were well-off and looked like free citizens.[8] Most of them had frost-bitten noses·and cheeks, and the continuous cold had a depressing effect on their spirits: they were not merry and spoke but little. Generally, they were honest in their business transactions. Only once did Mrs. Utovich have to shout when someone gave her a counterfeit bank-note.

"I don't want such trash. Do you think I am an idiot? Go to the steppe—to the Kirgiz with such money, not here, to me!"

As a rule, the business was transacted in a quiet, agreeable way, without any quarrels. Soon Mrozovetski even began to help because the old woman had difficulty adding. Then Sergey called her to the kitchen.

"My dear young master," she said as she went out, "the price is written on every article. Kindly take my place for a moment."

He remained there willingly. The work distracted his sad thoughts. He weighed and measured, gave the change, and was so busy that he heard neither the sleigh nor its bells, nor did he notice that Miss Marya was looking into the store. Behind her stood a young man.

"Aunt!" called she, but immediately corrected herself; and, without showing any surprise, added in her determined but sad voice:

"Grinya will bring the goods I have purchased. Will you be so kind as to unpack them?"

"Very well, madam," he answered, busily giving some change.

She went upstairs, followed by the stranger.

"By Jingo!" exclaimed the latter, laughing uproariously:

"Your brother had original taste! So that is his chosen

---

[8] As opposed to "serfs." Serfdom in Russia was abolished in stages, for most regions between 1861-4, but some regions came later: Georgia in 1871, for example, and Kalmykia only in 1892.

friend! What an original passenger—a real scarecrow! He looks like a cross between a country parish and helplessness. What a peach!"

"But you have hardly seen him," said Miss Marya.

"It's enough for me. I have particular talent as a physiognomist! One glance, and I know what a man is worth. In our century of great scientific progress and social changes, only he prospers who seizes upon things immediately. I have to!"

With great gallantry, he helped her out of her furs.

"Father is not yet back. He must have many patients."

They both entered the library, the young man behaving free and familiar, as a future husband should, and he fulfilled his part right zealously.

"Oh, you are cold! Poor little hands!" he said. "When will the time come for me to keep them idle?"

"It will never come," she answered.

"My dearest! Do not deprive me of my dreams! I dream of it day and night. I will make you a queen, a goddess, in my house. I will place you on an altar of worship and sentiment. You need not even give me orders—everything shall be done before you even speak! Pshaw! Before you think of it! I will not suffer any cloud of concern to darken that white forehead nor the least work to busy these little hands. Yes! I will do everything for you!"

Miss Marya only raised her eyebrows and smiled.

"Such a program is not for me. I take your words as a joke because you know me and know I couldn't accept such a part. I am not made to be a goddess but a helpmate to a man."

"So it seems to you. Life in Siberia changes everyone into some inferior being, and all work here like oxen. But we shall not live here when our happiness is complete. I shall not stay one day longer than I must. I will take my treasure back to Warsaw. There's a different life there—society, activity! Parties, and opera, and galleries! They would point their fingers at me if I allowed my wife to work! We are well-to-do people. I can afford to indulge myself in some luxury, such as an idle wife."

"You mustn't count me in for the luxury. Well, we had better not talk about it—it's so far off yet."

She took an account book from the desk and began to write in it. Mr. Shumski, standing before the mirror, adjusted his cravat and twisted up his mustache. Then he began to hum.

On hearing the humming, the young woman made a grimace, but he, in his excitement, did not notice. He only stopped humming on hearing the doctor's footsteps.

"I am glad you are here," said the doctor, addressing him. "What news? Your distilleries are working well?"

"I have fantastic results. I have brought the money for the rye. We are waiting for some more."

"Very well. I will go to Shchedrynsk tomorrow to get it. And how are my oxen?"[9]

"They grow fatter as you look at them."

"I cannot look after everything, but I rely on you in this and hope that everything is all right. Marya, please have supper served. Where is Mrozovetski?"

"He is busy in the store."

"Already? You soon found him something to do."

"It was not I. It must have been the aunt."

"Who should work if not he," said Shumski.

"Why, do you know him?"

"I have seen him; that is enough for me."

"Well, what do you think of him?"

"In two words—*anima vilis*!"[10]

"You are too hasty."

"That's my opinion, and to prove to you that I am not mistaken, I shall question him at the table. You will see, he will

____

[9] Calves bought from the Kirgiz in the autumn were taken to distilleries where they would be fed on the grain left over after fermentation.

[10] Anima vilis (latin): a cheap soul, a disposable soul

not understand anything finer, and I shall be able to skin him like a hippopotamus. I have a great talent for such things."

"Oh, you Gascon!" said the doctor indulgently. "What do they say about the fair in Kurhan?"

"They say business will be good. Have you anything for sale?"

"Only butter and oxen."

"You will make a pile."

"I shall spend it immediately, for I am going to purchase more oxen and put them in your distilleries to fatten. I must go to the steppe. Too much work for an old man like myself."

He said this with great self-satisfaction, but Shumski did not understand the real meaning of his words and said:

"You are working too hard. You ought to rest. You have plenty of money already."

"It is not a question of money. I have enough of that, as you say, but if I had nothing to do, I should think of my misfortune, and I cannot do that because I still have another child, and I must live and die in a Christian way. Marya, take this money for the rye and put it down in the books. Here is your receipt, sir."

At this moment, Mrs. Utovich announced that dinner was ready. Shumski helped her set the table, teasing her all the while. He joked about with Father Ubish and filled the house with laughter, which sounded strange, remembering their recent loss, but these sturdy people became accustomed to his liveliness, and perhaps they liked him on account of his joyful disposition.

Miss Marya found a moment to run downstairs to the store, where Mrozovetski was unpacking the goods.

"It was too bad of my aunt to make you work so soon," said the girl.

"I am glad of it. Otherwise, I should have nothing to do," he answered sadly. "I haven't worked for a long time. I am surprised to think that I can be useful. In my country, I was accustomed to seeing how people waited around for any kind of work.”

“You will not see it here! But enough for today. Let us be going to dinner. We have a guest—our countryman also.”

“Is it Mr. Shumski?”

“Yes. Do you know him?”

“No. But Mrs. Utovich told me that he is a superintendent of several distilleries. I thought I might perhaps get a position through him. I am a mechanical engineer.”

“You could try,” she answered, shrugging her shoulders, which, with her, meant dissatisfaction.

They entered the dining room, and the doctor shook hands with him cordially. Shumski saluted him from afar. While drinking vodka and eating caviare before dinner, they came to a skirmish at once.

Mrozovetski, tired and bashful, did not retort with a single joke.

“What are you going to do here? Conquer Siberia, hey? I am sure you are a specialist. Did they not appreciate your talents in Europe?”

“I do know how to work,” answered the newcomer timidly, and his face did not express any discomfort at such a humiliating examination.”

“And in what branch have you been the star, hey? Parents spoiled you, probably? It must be dreadful for you here?”

“I have no parents.”

“How, then, could you come into this world? From wind or water?”

Mrozovetski looked steadily at Shumski and replied slowly.

“I don’t know about the way. I assume there is only one. I graduated from an Institute of Technology.”

At this, everybody smiled. Miss Marya glanced at him. Shumski was right, his was a slow mind. Why did Antony love and esteem him so much? For his docility and probity, assuredly.

"I am sure you studied well; have a splendid memory and think quickly. No doubt you did two years a year."

"I never knew it was permitted. Perhaps there are such schools. I took the usual seven years to complete the Gymnasium."

"Oh! How well you calculate! Seven classes—seven years. Regular mathematical head! And how old were you when you finished at the Gymnasium?"

"Seventeen."

"Well, well. Ordinarily, at that age, one is a perfect ass!"

Here Father Ubish created a diversion by asking to have the beetroot passed.

"Beetroot. I want some beetroot," he whined like a capricious child.

They gave him some, and then Mrozovetski said:

"I am sure you are from Warsaw?"

"How did you guess it?"

"I worked in a factory in Warsaw. I know the people—they are a jolly lot."

"You were in Warsaw! How did you get along there? I am sure you were lionized by women and fought over by employers!"

"No, I worked one year in a railroad machine shop."

"You held the position of a director, yes?"

"No, a mechanical engineer."

"Ho-ho, and direct from Gymnasium. It's very smart indeed."

"I was already through with my military service. It was about two years ago."

"And now I am sure you will tell us something about women!"

"Nothing of great interest. Everybody passes through it, studies, gets some position, and gets married."

26

"Then you are married. I am overawed!" and he bowed ironically.

Mrozovetski saluted him with dignity.

"Thank you, but that will only be necessary later. For the moment, I am merely engaged to marry."

"Then send her my respects. I am sorry not to be able to make her acquaintance. Then you contemplate building a nest here?"

"God knows," answered the newcomer laconically. "I should like to find some occupation here. Perhaps in your distilleries, there might be some position for me?"

"Ah, my dear sir, having profited by sad experiences, we ask for qualifications, testimonials, diplomas, trials, proofs. We need specialists. Self-made men don't pay."

"That is true," assented Mrozovetski, "but up to now, wherever I have worked, people have been satisfied with me. Only the economic depression in our country has driven me here. I have diplomas and certificates, and if your employer so wishes, I can produce them."

"Oh, my employer is not accustomed to deciding anything without me. Well, I will remember your request. Perhaps I shall be able to make some use of you."

The doctor and his daughter took no part in the conversation. They did not care for this kind of joking, and only Mrs. Utovich laughed from time to time, or the priest burst into untimely idiotic laughter.

At length, they rose from the table. Mrozovetski, embarrassed, prepared to go to his room, not wishing to intrude upon the family gathering, but the doctor called him.

"Won't you join me in a smoke?" he asked.

"No, thank you," came the evasive reply.

He was an inveterate smoker but was ashamed to smoke someone else's tobacco when he was too poor to buy any himself.

He remained with them awhile and then went

downstairs. The old woman was glad to see him in the store again and immediately yielded him her place. She had plenty to do in the kitchen. He sat in the shop patiently. He saw Shumski leave; he saw that Miss Marya was busy about the house. At length, toward evening, the doctor came down.

"Well, how is business?" he asked, sitting down beside him.

"Very good, as far as I can judge."

"Business was better when I had the only store in the village, but now there are three others. Even we have competition."

Some customers came in—among them some dignified old farmers. They began to talk.

"So, Casimir Stanislavovich, you have brought another son from Europe? Well, this is a smart boy. He will be stronger than the other. With his help, you will be able to do more business."

The doctor shook his head.

"This is not my son, but a countryman come to visit us."

"Don't allow him to go back. He must help you. Take him for your son since God has taken the other. Drive that fellow with the red beard away and give your daughter to this man: then you will be a powerhouse! You are old and can't look after everything, and the girl, though she is smart and hardworking, can't do as well as a boy. This one looks smart; he will be a man."

"That's not the way we do business, Nikita Ivanovich."

"Why not? It's an honest business."

He slapped Mrozovetski on the shoulder familiarly and added:

"Why should you go back? Our country is good. You listen to Casimir Stanislavovich, and you will be all right."

He paid for the goods he had purchased and went out. The doctor was silent and stood looking through the window. Mrozovetski was embarrassed and, to regain his composure,

28

began to make out his accounts.

Miss Marya brought a lamp and helped him. She did this quickly and skilfully, hardly speaking a word. The day ended. She asked their guest to go upstairs with her father while she locked the store.

Mrozovetski went for a moment to his room, then returned to the dining-room, and gazed through the window at the empty street. The lamps were not yet lighted, and he thought no one was near until he heard Miss Marya's voice in the doctor's room.

"Father, don't weep. You must not weep. My dearest, I know I cannot replace him, but you know how I love you!"

"I remember that I have you. I remember it well. You see, I am calm during the day, but this hour of dusk—it belongs to us. You sometimes weep too. Let me then rid my eyes of the fire that burns them. How long is it now since—?"

"Seventeen days. I wonder how we have survived."

"You have become so frail, so thin. Only one-half of you remains. You can't sleep?"

"No, father."

"We don't work enough. We must work more, more! Work will help us forget our sorrow! Do you remember the times when he used to sing to us?"

"Yes, I remember. He read aloud to us, too, or told us about Europe. Now, how long and tedious the evenings are. My Lord, how dreadful it must be for him in that foreign cemetery."

There was a long silence. The girl laid her head on her father's shoulder, and his tears flowed onto her dark head. A soft sobbing filled the room. It was already dark.

Suddenly, Mrs. Utovich brought in a lamp into the dining room.

"Where are the master and miss? I am going to serve tea."

"Can I help you?" asked Mrozovetski.

"Oh, yes, thank you. Sergey is gone, snuck out to the dram shop again. I hope that drunkard will freeze to death tonight. Come to the kitchen. The samovar[11] is too heavy for me to lift."

After a while, Mrozovetski brought in a steaming samovar, and the lamps were lighted in the doctor's office.

Miss Marya sat in the dining room, quiet as usual, a little gloomy and absorbed in her work.

"I see aunt has dominated you altogether," she said, addressing the young man.

"Since I can be of service to her, I can eat your bread with a better conscience."

"It's Antony's bread. You are his guest," Miss Marya responded testily.

"I beg your pardon. I did not mean to offend. He knew me and knew that I could misspeak sometimes, but he would know that I meant well."

"It's too bad," she answered softly.

The doctor entered the dining room.

"If we do not have the blizzard tomorrow, I am going to Shchedrynsk to buy some rye," he said.

They sat down at the table.

"May I ask you where Shishkin, the owner of the distilleries, lives?" asked Mrozovetski.

"In Kurhan—when he is at home. Do you think seriously of trying to get a position here?"

"I shall be only too glad if he takes me."

"Have you the necessary qualifications for such a position?"

The young man pulled out a large pocketbook and took from it some papers.

"Here is my diploma from the Institute of Technology, and here is a certificate from a factory in Warsaw."

"That's splendid. Today at dinner, you were so shy in

---

[11] A samovar (literally "self-brewer") is a metal container traditionally used to brew and keep tea hot.

answering Shumski that I wondered if we had to do with an amateur."

"I answered in the same way that Shumski questioned me. He likes to joke. Why should I spoil his pleasure."

Miss Marya looked at him, much surprised. He was speaking seriously, as usual, and his face wore the same indifferent expression. She began to suspect that this air of indifference hid something quite different.

The doctor went through all the papers.

"They are splendid. People with such qualifications are needed here."

"One must have good luck in everything, and until now, I have never in my life had any luck."

"Tell us something about yourself, won't you?"

"It will not be very interesting."

"On the contrary. You are Antony's friend. We want to know you."

"I will tell you then if you like," he answered simply.

"If you will permit me," said Mrs. Utovich, "I will listen also. I am sure you will say something about our country. One always wants to hear the news."

They were all sitting at the dining room table. The doctor played solitaire, and the women sewed. Mrozovetski replenished the fire and began thus:

"Until I was nine years old, I was—very rich, I think, you would say. My father had a large estate in Podlasie, Promieniev: land, forest, lakes, fish ponds. We were only two children, myself and a sister a couple of years younger. I don't remember my mother.

"When I was nine years old, we lost everything: our father, our estate, our wealth, even our good name. I didn't know about it then, but later on, they told me that my father had debts and that many people had lost money through him. The estate of Promieniev was purchased by Burski, my father's friend. We remained under his care, my sister and I. He was a hard man—avaricious and misanthropical; but he gave us that which the poor need—education. That, and a certain hardening for the battle of life. The food was poor, the clothing rough, and the house was always cold. We became accustomed to all kinds of hardship and misery, which were shared with us by his own daughter, his only child, and heiress to a very large fortune. Burski was very wealthy indeed!

"Two years passed in this way, then he sent me to school. Even there, I was obliged to be satisfied with the bare necessities of life, as only my board was paid for. When I outgrew my clothes, I did not dare ask for new ones; so, beginning with the third grade,[12] I began to tutor, and with this and some copying, I got along somehow.

"I almost always spent my vacations back in our parts, in Podlasie: in Promieniev, or at a nearby estate of Vistitski, my mother's relative. My sister, Valka, who grew up with young Miss Burski, did not complain. She had almost forgotten the better times of her childhood.

"When I was in the fifth grade, Burski stopped paying my board, owing to 'hard times,' as he said. I don't know how it was with him, but it really went bad with me, and had it not been for the help of some good friends, I could never have finished the Gymnasium. When, after two years of hard work, I brought him my diploma, he said nothing. He did not care for me one jot. He kept my sister because she worked for him, performing the work of a housekeeper without pay.

"I had no one to go to for advice, and there was no use in my returning there again, as people were ill-disposed toward me on account of my father. After resting for a couple of months, I went to St Petersburg. During that journey, I met Antony, and his acquaintance was a blessing to me."

Here Mrozovetski stopped, fearing he had said too

----

[12] Third grade of the Gymnasium: the boy would have been about 13 years old

much. He glanced at his listeners. They shuddered, but after a while, the doctor arose, approached the fire-place, and, seating himself near Mrozovetski, said:

"Go on. Tell us everything."

"He and I became acquainted on the train. I lacked the money to continue my journey and was in such despair that I determined to beg for it. I approached him, but I could not beg, and I began to cry. He did not ask me any questions but said:

"'You great baby. If you cry like this about some stupid money, how you will cry after a love heartbreak! Don't bother yourself. I have enough for us both. Stick to me, and you will be all right.'

"Since that time, he looked after me like an older brother, and as long as I live, there will be no moment in my life that I shall not bless him."

And he began to weep.

The doctor took his head in both hands and pressed it to his breast.

Now Miss Marya understood why her brother had loved this modest, slow man. It was for his simple soul; for his simple sentiments; for his faithfulness and gratitude.

In the meantime, the young man overcame his emotion and continued:

"We shared a room, and he paid my expenses for two years. Then I got a scholarship. In my last year at school, I was so well off that I was able to save a hundred roubles and wanted to pay him back. That was the only time he got angry with me.

"'Are you blind?' he said. 'Don't you see how many comrades of ours are in misery? And you, long-eared ass, you bring me this money? Get out! Don't you know that Zatorski is sick in bed and that Mirecki eats only once in three days? Go to them, you fool!'

"After that day, I knew where to repay the debts I owed him.

"He finished his studies and started a practice in Warsaw.

I got my diploma and joined him. We loved each other so much that we could not live separated, so we took rooms together again. I found a situation with a salary of over a thousand roubles. But such good fortune, coming after long years of misery, turned my head, and I began to live fast. Antony noticed it; he scolded me; he advised me; but, seeing that I took no notice of it, one day, he said:

"'Listen. You have a good position. Marry as soon as you can. Otherwise, you will become a good-for-nothing.'

"When he said that, I remembered Zosha Burski, and I determined to see her at once. I went to Promieniev. There I found everything as I had left it. The house was half in ruins, and the old man was more stingy than ever. Zosha had grown to be a quiet, timid young woman. Just the right sort for me. I told my plans to Valka, my sister, but she looked at me and said

"'No way!'

"'Why?' I asked.

"'First, because her father will never give her to you. And, second, because you cannot marry the daughter of the man who murdered your father.'

"I looked at her in astonishment, and she continued:

"'I learned it not long since, and I wished to write to you about it, but I decided to wait until we see each other in person. Do you remember that our father had a coachman named Thomas?"

"'Yes, he did.'

"'Well, that coachman saw our father, while he was already very ill, give Burski the money with which to pay off his debts. Our father had just inherited Aunt Vistitski's estate, and some cash came into his hands. Burski took the money and went to Warsaw but told the creditors that our father was insolvent and purchased all their claims himself for half their value. He thought our father would soon die and kept everything secret. But, by accident, one of the creditors succeeded in seeing our father and disclosed to him Burski's shameful scheme. Then our

34

father, though standing over his grave, went to the city and, after learning the truth there, died in his hotel room from a stroke.'

"'On hearing this, I became frantic,' Valka continued. 'You have forgotten everything while at your studies. But I, living here, forlorn and miserable, through Burski's misdeeds, heard all that people said. I carefully gathered their reminiscences of our father. I gathered and preserved our injuries in my heart to tell them to you when you became a man. You must vindicate our father's name and crush this man who has been the cause of all our misery. I have known this for a long time, but I did not wish to disturb your studies, so I suffered and waited alone."

"Where is this coachman?" I asked.

"He is dead. He took five hundred roubles for his silence and remained silent until his last moment. But when he was dying, he sent for me, not wishing to go to the grave with this sin on his mind."

"'This can't be true!" I said. 'Uncle Vistitski was then Marshal of Nobility.[13] He would have defended us.'

"'Perhaps he would have done it if Burski, acting under power of attorney for our father, had not given him our aunt's estate. Uncle Vistitski was afraid that he would have to take care of us; that we should become a burden to him; and he forced Burski, by his power as Marshal of Nobility, to bring us up. This Burski did, but... we have not cost him much.'

"'But give me some proof!' I said. 'A dead man is no witness.'

"'There is another witness who is still alive, a Dr. Drozdowski, who attended on our father.'"

"'Where is he?'

---

[13] Marshal of the nobility: an institution of noble self-government dating back to the times of the Polish Commonwealth and continued under Russian occupation. County marshals were supposed to preside over county assemblies, keep genealogical books, and watch over the lifestyle of noblemen so that it did not deviate from accepted norms.

"'No one knows. There were disturbances,[14] and he disappeared without a trace.'

"'Then we can only bring our case to the court of the Last Judgment,' I answered sadly. 'Poor Zosha!'

"'Not so poor as you think. Young Vistitski wishes to marry her. The Vistitskis are near bankruptcy, but Burski cannot possibly find a more titled husband for his daughter. You must give up all idea of marrying her. Let their kind stay together.'

"I gave up, full of bitterness. I regretted Zosha, and I hated Burski more than ever. I am not vengeful by nature, but in this case, I should have liked to crush him. I went to see him and told him that I was going to take my sister away with me. He demurred at this because she worked for him for nothing. Then I said to him:

"'You have taken from us our father's good name, our wealth, and our social position. The girl has paid with hard work for the bread you have given her. Now I have made a position for myself and will take care of her henceforth. I will leave you alone, and God shall judge you.'

"'He sprang at me like a wild beast, but I threw him off and left him. I took Valka with me and went back to Warsaw with her.

"With that, my misfortunes began again. The factory owners were obliged to restructure, and I lost my position, and soon after, Antony went away to Siberia. I went from factory to factory searching for work, while my sister earned money by sewing. In that way, a year and six months passed, and the misery we endured during that time used up all our reserve stock of strength and faith.

"At the moment when everything was darkest, Burski offered to help us, but we refused. We hated him so much that

---

[14] Probably the national uprising 1861-1863, in the wake of th4 fall of which a lot of Polish nobility was sent into exile in Siberia

we felt we would rather die than accept anything from him. Finally, I found work and saved some money—and Antony summoned me here. After consulting Valka, I determined to try my luck in Siberia, and Valka had an idea that perhaps beyond the Urals, I could find the missing witness, this Dr. Drozdowski. In the autumn, having set aside five hundred roubles, I set out, leaving my sister with my fiancee. Both girls had good positions in a store. But it seems that my ill luck followed me, for you know the condition in which Miss Marya found me on the steppe.

"That's all."

Mrozovetski became silent. The doctor and his daughter were also silent for a while, in deep thought. Only Father Ubish, who during the whole time had been building card houses, said complainingly:

"You build, and build, and build, and that which you build falls down."

Mrs. Utovich, folding her hands in her lap, said:

"When you left the country, was the grass still green, and were the trees covered with leaves?"

"The grass was still green in the fields, but the trees had turned red and yellow and lost half their leaves."

"My Lord! My Lord! For twenty years, I have not seen our autumn. Oh, the climate here! In the spring, they sow quickly and gather quickly, for the cold begins in late August and lasts until May! And where are the trees? Elms, oaks! Here there are only birches and pine trees. Antony brought us a branch of lilac. We planted it on the south side of the house, and every winter, we cover it with straw and manure to keep it from freezing, but it seems to me that the flowers do not smell as sweetly as they do in our country. Have you not brought any souvenirs with you?"

"I had some seeds and dried flowers, but the thieves in Tobolsk stole everything. I have only a medallion with the Holy Virgin from Ostra Brama."

"Oh, I have a similar one, and the family also has one. We treasure them."

The doctor and his daughter exchanged glances. They understood each other without a word being spoken. The girl nodded, and the doctor stretched out his hand and laid it on Mrozovetski's head.

"On this penitential road, God has taken from me the hope and aim of my life—my son," said the doctor solemnly. "Perhaps in taking pity, He then sent you to me. Remain with us as a brother and a countryman. Will you?"

"No need to ask me. I will give you my best in your service," said Mrozovetski with emotion.

"Very well. Now, I would ask you a favor—you must excuse an old man—I shall call you Antony. May I?" whispered the doctor with quivering lips.

Mrozovetski said nothing but pressed the doctor's hand. Then he rose and approached Miss Marya timidly.

"Thank you!" he whispered.

She raised her eyes and silently held out her hand with dignity. He knew, from the pressure of her hand, that her father's action had not pleased her, and he felt humiliated, thinking he had appeared to take advantage of the old man's emotion and had too easily agreed to play a part, which by right, belonged to Shumski. At once, all his joy was quenched, and all warmth disappeared. Again he felt a stranger to them—more than a stranger: an intruder and a foe, notwithstanding that his intentions were pure.

He retreated and knew not what to say when Father Ubish began talking about his card houses.

"That they fall when I build them badly, I can understand, but that they also fall when I build them well! Why? I will not build anymore." At that moment, the dogs began to bark in the courtyard, and Mrs. Utovich jumped in her chair.

"I am sure Sergey is coming back. What a dreadful

drunkard. Now he will be sick again for three days."

The doctor rose and said:

"Someone must go and see what the matter is." He looked at Mrozovetski and said:

"Will you go and take the old drunkard to his room?"

Mrozovetski went downstairs.

In the courtyard, Sergey was lying drunk in the snow, with the dogs jumping on him and snipping at him joyfully. He was talking to them.

"Noo-noo, Putsik! Noo-noo, Mutsik! Down, down you Sibiraks! You want some cutlets? Hein?"

He tried to rise. Mrozovetski took him to the kitchen, where the warmth soon caused him to become motionless and stiff.

"I am sick," he said and fell asleep.

The young man went to his room. All the other inmates of the house had retired. The wanderer sat down on the bed of his dead friend and began to think. Now he regretted having accepted the doctor's invitation. He was downcast and sorrowful. The women were against him; he would be obliged to meet Shumski frequently, and the situation was bound to be unpleasant. Why did he agree? Would it not be better to go blindly forward in his struggle for bread than to remain here? He was tempted to go at once and then, after obtaining employment, return and explain. But he was ashamed of such thoughts. Raising his eyes, he saw a photograph of his friend, who seemed to look reproachfully at him. That sight comforted him, and he sighed deeply.

"I can't refuse your father!" he whispered. "Let come what will. I will close my lips and suffer."

He did not sleep much that night. He washed his only shirt for the coming Sunday and then brushed and mended his clothes as best he could. If these would only last for some time— at least until the summer—then he could sell his sheepskin coat, and then... Well, during his whole life, he had not had an answer for this "then," and still, he somehow survived.

The next day, the whole European colony[15] gathered in the doctor's room, and Antony became acquainted with his countrymen. There were ten of them: old people, nearing their life's end, and young ones, either brought up here or newcomers. The majority, especially the elderly ones, expressed in their looks and voices dull resignation and quietude. The others looked fearless; they were noisy and wild. All were poor. Some were small tradesmen; others were clerks in stores. The elders lived on a few roubles sent them monthly by their relatives. As it was Sunday, they were dressed decently, and everyone who entered asked the same question,

"How is the Father today?"

"Very well!" answered Mrs. Utovich from the kitchen, where, in place of "indisposed" Sergey, she was obliged to prepare their dinner.

That day Father Ubish was remarkably solemn and clear-minded. From early morning he trotted about the house, reciting his Latin prayers, rearranged the ribbons in a worn-out missal, and did not speak to anyone. The visitors spoke in low voices, greeted the host, gathered in the dining room, and looked at the closed doors of the doctor's office.

"Thank God, we shall have a mass!" they whispered in relief.

Every Sunday, they came in uncertainty—Father Ubish had fits of melancholy, and sometimes strange fancies took possession of him. At such times he did not wish to read the mass, and they prayed without him. They had not had a mass for three weeks, but that day the priest seemed cooperative.

After they had waited for a while, he entered the doctor's office. Behind him was a temporary altar, and on it, the image of the Holy Virgin of Częstochowa.[16]

---

[15] European colony: here the author means Polish exiles
[16] A widely revered icon of Virgin Mary

"Does anyone require confession?" he asked clearly.

Several old men followed him into the improvised chapel, and Miss Marya entered the dining room and asked for Mr. Rogovski.

"He hasn't come. Shishkin sent him to Shchedrynsk."

"Is there anybody among you who could replace him?"

"Nobody remembers the words of the prayers," some youngster replied.

"Could you attend the priest?" she asked Mrozovetski.

"Go, Antony!" the doctor said.

Only now, the whole colony noticed him, for, as usual, he stood aside.

"Who is he?" they asked the doctor.

"My son's friend," he answered abruptly.

There was no time to ask more, for, at that moment, the bell rang, and they all went into the chapel.

They drew old prayer books from their pockets.

They heard the mass, kneeling and praying so loud that their voices often drowned out the ritual's Latin words. Father Ubish seemed quite changed. He was solemn and dignified, with fire in his usually watery eyes, and his movements were full of unction.

From the kitchen, Mrs. Utovich rushed in and, kneeling down, said,

"Oh, Lord, give him eternal rest."

This she repeated again and again.

Evidently, there were many souls for whom she prayed eternal rest.

In the end, the priest intoned the hymn, *Sub tuum praesidium.*[17]

Everybody closed their books, and looking at the holy picture, they sang this by heart, and their faces—wild and degraded by misery or sharpened by illness—were lit up and

---

[17] Latin: "Under your protection"

ennobled with enthusiasm. The priest rose, took off his church robes, and, returning to his everyday persona, almost ran to the kitchen to fetch his coffee. After he left, one by one, they went into the dining room. At first, they were dignified, then the youngsters began to talk aloud about the coming fair, and soon a general hubbub filled the room.

Mrozovetski noticed that, contrary to the duty of a host, the doctor did not mingle in the conversation. He sat at the table and looked thoughtfully at his guests. Finally, he called Mrozovetski and said softly:

"Be kind enough to leave the room for a while. You may listen if you like, but I must respect their sensitivities. I have something unpleasant to say to them. You understand, don't you?"

When he had left the room, the old man asked his guests:

"Why is Rogovski absent?"

A big fellow named Lukovski laughed.

"Well, you scolded him last Sunday, and he swore he would never come here again."

"Was I not right?"

"Certainly, you were right," answered Lukovski, "but everyone has his own pride."

"His pride ought to make him act correctly. And if you acknowledge that I am right, why then do you act in the same way as he? Instead of working, you all gamble and lose your money, and when your money is gone, you cheat Shishkin."

"We are not thieves," grumbled Lukovski.

"He who walks in a marsh should know that he can sink very deep in the mire, and he should retreat as soon as he soils his shoes. Until now, everybody here respected us. We should cherish this good opinion. By your misdeeds, you are not only injuring yourselves personally, but you are bringing your nation into bad repute, and we command you to respect your nation—we, who are all of the same blood. If you are upright and intelligent men, you will understand me and act accordingly.

We must keep guard over each other because we have no source from which to draw moral refreshment. Tell Rogovski to come back to his countrymen."

Lukovski, ashamed of himself, was silent, and the doctor turned to another young man who was dressed like a Russian peasant.

"And you, Rudnicki. Is what they say true, that you are going to marry the daughter of the peasant Iliya from Nagorna?"

"I was only joking," explained Rudnicki.

"If it was a joke, it was a stupid one, and if you were thinking of marrying a peasant's daughter, I call it a shame!"

"One can easily lose his mind from loneliness and boredom," grumbled Rudnicki.

An old man with a thin, sickly face said:

"Tobol flows not far from your home. Why don't you drown yourself if loneliness eats you up."

"Go easy, Valenty," the doctor said to him. And then turned to the young man again:

"Rudnicki, when you are lonely, come and see us in the evening. I have some books, and now you will find a young Mrozovetski here. Come, I pray you. You will always be welcome."

Rudnicki, embarrassed, twisted his fingers and said,

"But I should like to marry."

At this, all burst out laughing, and an old man said:

"Why don't you come to see me then?"

"Will you give me your daughter?"

"Why not? I did not bring her up for myself but for one of you fellows."

"Why not for me!"

"Or for me!"

"Or for me!" several shouted at once.

"Hey, hey, I was first!" cried Rudnicki.

Evidently, the doctor had nothing more to say, for he did

not stop the noise but began to talk with Valenty, and then Mrs. Utovich entered and commenced to lay the table. The host called Mrozovetski and introduced him to the countrymen. After a short time, they treated him cordially, in their rough fashion, like an old acquaintance. They asked him about the far West, about the trees and water, and about people long since dead. The old men had not forgotten politics, and with Marcinkowski, the father of the much-desired girl, Mrozovetski redrew the map of Europe seven times, each time more fantastically than the last.

They ate their dinner with the appetites of wolves and then began to leave the house.

When the door closed behind the last one, the doctor put his hand on the young man's shoulder and said:

"See how difficult it is to plant a branch cut from the trunk, how difficult it is to preserve it green. And all of them have the same thought: 'Go back!' Go back, indeed! And to a place where they were worse off."

"Don't you wish to go back?" timidly asked the young man.

"I must stay here. Don't you see? For how many years have they known this house? Where would they go on a Sunday? To the dram shop. No, I must remain here."

As he spoke thus, his eyes, full of quiet resignation, were fixed on the window pane, covered with snow.

And Mrozovetski assented softly, "Yes, you must remain here."

CHAPTER III
With the Kirgiz

EARLY the next morning, the doctor awakened Mrozovetski.

"We will go out on the steppe," he said.

The young man, not being accustomed to ask questions, dressed quickly and glanced at the thermometer, which registered only twenty degrees.

"Remarkably mild winter," said Doctor Gostinski during breakfast. "We have quite a way to go—about fifty versts. Marya will take Grinya and the horses, and we will go with Andryanek. I wonder that he is not here yet."

At that moment, a man of gigantic stature appeared in the doorway. He took off his cap, crossed himself, made several bows before a holy image, and after familiarly greeting those present, sat down at the table.

"Now you meet Antony Stefanovich," said the doctor.

"Yes. My father told me you had your countryman with you, but I didn't have time to come and make his acquaintance yet. I like the look of him, and maybe we will become friends if he is smart and a huntsman. Have you a rifle?"

"No."

"Buy one then. I will let you have powder and ball. In

our country, there is plenty to do in winter, as well as in the summer: partridges, ducks, bielaks, galanduks. Now there is plenty of fish. Come and see us so that we may become better acquainted. We were friends with the dead man."

"I will send him to you when we have more time. Now, before the fair, we are very busy," said the doctor.

"Of course. Well, I have had my tea. Let us be going."

"Do you think we shall find the Kirgiz near the lake?"

"And where else should that vermin be? There are usually about twenty yurts[18] during the winter there."

"Then let us go, in God's name."

"One minute," said Andryanek, glancing at Mrozovetski.

"He must not go with us in that state. His felt boots are worn out, and his tulub[19] is too light. You must dress warmer, otherwise, we shall have trouble with you on the steppe."

"I am all right," said Mrozovetski, coloring hotly at this reference to his poor clothing. But the peasant laughed.

"Don't blush like a girl! If you haven't another coat, take mine. I brought three along. And don't worry about being poor. You will be rich someday."

At this speech, Mrozovetski wished that the ground would open beneath his feet and swallow him. The doctor and Miss Marya looked at him.

"I should have thought of it!" exclaimed the old man. "Wait! Wait! Marya, give me the key to the trunk."

"I will fetch what is necessary," answered the girl in her usual imperturbable, tranquil manner.

She brought a new coat and felt boots, and it seemed to Mrozovetski that she mentally made a note of the value of the articles as she handed them to him. He dressed without a word while the doctor grumbled:

---

[18] A large tent of the Eurasian steppe
[19] sheepskin coat

"Must I take care of you like a child? Such stupid pride and independence!"

They finally found themselves seated in Andryanek's sleigh and started off like the wind.

"Where are we going?" asked Mrozovetski.

"To the Kirgiz, to buy some oxen off them. In three weeks there is a big fair in Kurhan. I shall slaughter all the oxen I have had fattened in the distilleries for the fair and put new oxen in their place. I shall buy them today, and you will take them home because I will be busy with the grain."

They drove on over the clean, bare steppe, the peasant whistling joyfully.

"How do the Kirgiz keep their cattle during the winter?"

"They pasture them."

"On the snow?"

"Yes, you shall see. Look, here, a herd has passed. We are near the yurts."

In fact, the snow was trampled, and here and there, the stems of last year's herbs could be seen.

"Here, some horses passed," remarked Andryanek. "The horses go ahead," explained the doctor, "and break the ice and snow with their hooves. Then come the cattle, and what remains is eaten by the sheep."

"And they do not give them anything else to eat?"

"No. The weaker ones die during the winter, but the stronger, and the majority of them, survive."

"Here are your oxen!" exclaimed Andryanek. A herd of animals was feeding on the bare steppe. The cattle were not large, but they were broad and so emaciated that one could count their bones. They were grazing on the dried-up stems, bushes, and blackened remnants of the herbs. Behind the herd, a few Kirgiz sat motionless on their small horses. The doctor inspected the oxen and called to the herdsmen, showing them a piece of silver money.

They came at once and began to mumble and point

behind them to where, on the far horizon, some smoke was visible.

"Whose are these oxen?" asked the doctor. They pointed out different herds of cattle, saying:

"This belongs to Beygabul-Buka; that one to Schynzdey-Kyesdeyeff."

"I know both of them. Let us be going."

They went in the direction of the smoke. It became more and more distinct, but nothing else indicated a human habitation there. Around the freshwater lake, the wind had heaped snow on herbs and weeds, and the evaporation of this snow was what had looked like smoke from afar. Further on, they approached the yurts, and around one of them, Mrozovetski perceived piles of blackened bones of the cattle who had perished—the trophy of the winter. Among these skeletons, which were more or less bare of meat, some living beings moved about. They were the children of the Kirgiz, scraping with their knives the remainder of the frozen meat and eating it voraciously. As soon as they noticed the strangers, they hid within the pile.

The yurts were round. Thick felt constituted the interior walls, while the exterior was of snow. The smoke escaped by a single opening, which also served as a door and was covered by a piece of felt. The doctor, being familiar with their customs, entered the first yurt, followed by Mrozovetski. Andryanek stayed with the horses.

Thick darkness and choking smoke were the first things that impressed one on entering the yurt, and the stench was so strong that Antony staggered and wished to retreat. But hearing the doctor's voice, he mechanically repeated after him the words of greeting and began to look around. Little by little, his eyes became accustomed to the darkness, and he could distinguish different objects in the room. He was standing as though in a box, narrower at the top and with dark sides. Under his feet was a felt carpet, and in front of him, a fire of dried manure, over

48

which was suspended a large iron pot filled with kumis.[20] Near the walls, on a pile of felt, was a human figure, and two others could be seen sitting near the fire, looking curiously at the newcomers.

The doctor opened the conversation, having first seated himself.

"I greet you, Beygabul-Buka."

"Be healthy," answered one of the seated figures without moving.

He was the owner of the yurt: an elderly man, feeble and sallow, wearing a round black cap on his clean-shaven head and dressed in a long fur cloak. Having greeted them, he mumbled something in his own language, and immediately those seated at the fire handed the doctor and Mrozovetski glasses of kumis. Probably they were Beygabul-Buka's wives. Then they approached the young man and began to mumble, making many gestures. Of this mumbling, he could understand only one word, "bread." He put his hand into his pocket and drew forth a large piece of cake that Mrs. Utovich had given him for his luncheon. This he gave them, and they pulled it from his hands, divided it, and devoured it in the twinkling of an eye. Becoming bolder, they began to examine him, touch his clothes and express astonishment and wonder.

In the meantime, the doctor explained his business, and the bargaining began. They did not use many words. The doctor put before him the Chinese balls used for counting, and he indicated with them his price. The Kirgiz thought, looked, and added two balls, which the doctor rejected after a while. In that way, they repeated the same movement like two automatons.

Finally, the Kirgiz began to praise his own oxen.

The doctor shrugged his shoulders and said, "They are

------

[20] Kumis is a mare dairy product similar to kefir, but because mare's milk contains more sugars than cow's or goat's milk, when fermented, kumis has a higher, though still mild, alcohol content.

not oxen; they are skins!" and he again rejected the balls.

Then he treated the Kirgiz to tobacco, and as they smoked their pipes, only the sound of the wooden balls was heard. In that way, they busied themselves for about an hour. Two Kirgiz entered the yurt, and the women began to skin a sheep carcass. The scene grew animated, and from beneath the pile of felts, the heads of children began to appear. The newcomers were also served kumis. The doctor pulled a bottle of vodka from his bag.

Mrozovetski approached him and looked at the balls. The difference was now one rouble.

"This scarecrow is rich," said the doctor softly. "Every year, I purchase from him two hundred oxen. He has horses and sheep in the same proportion."

"How many are you buying now?"

"Sixty, at six roubles each."

"Are these people honest?"

"They are thieves and are cheated a hundred times themselves by others."

Beygabul-Buka mumbled for a few minutes with his neighbors and finally divided the difference in two. He was in great haste to get a drink. The doctor first wrote an agreement, having brought in his bag everything necessary for writing, and a candle, which, in the bad air of the yurt, burned very badly, and gave barely enough light to distinguish the clumsy letters in which Beygabul-Buka signed his name to the agreement. This was witnessed by Mrozovetski and Kirgiz Schynyiney. Only after this was accomplished did they drink the vodka. The purchasers then left the foul air of the yurt to breathe the fresh air of the steppe. The doctor laughed at Mrozovetski's shocked mien, and Andryanek swore at those "dirty and stinking creatures."

"Every country has its customs," said the old man. "In Europe, all the hard and dirty work is done by the poor, by miserable employees. Here everybody is equal. The same hands which count money by the thousand skin the sheep and measure rendered fat at the fair. Nobody wonders or jokes at seeing a rich man taking care of his own herd, and nobody envies him his money. His farmhand sits at the same table with him, and he cannot understand that he might be inferior in any respect to his master.

"'My master is rich,' he says to himself. 'Well, I, too, can become rich with any luck.' In Europe, even my clerk would not pay a visit to Beygabul, but here, when I have need of him, I visit him myself. Here, one must gather with one's own hands the kopeks as well as the roubles. Only in that way can one make a fortune here, for here life is still primitive, the people are simple, and Nature is in a virgin state."

They entered the sleigh and started homeward.

"Tomorrow, we will divide the work," continued the doctor. "I will go to Shchedrynsk to purchase grain, and you will go round to the distilleries and check up on my oxen."

The young man, after a moment of silence, said with hesitation:

"Would it not be better for me to go and buy the grain?"

"Why?"

"Perhaps Shumski will not like me to inspect his work."

"What do you care about Shumski? You are doing your duty, and you mustn't care about anything or anybody."

"As you say."

It was evening when they returned home. The doctor was called away directly to see a sick man. Mrozovetski was received by the women. It seemed to him that Miss Marya looked at his clothing inquisitively. He undressed immediately, placing the borrowed clothes in the dining room.

Marya noticed this. She looked into his eyes, and her glance became somber. She rose and, without saying a word, put the clothing away. That evening she did not speak to him. From merely indifferent, they were fast becoming foes. Conversation with Mrs. Utovich was not very animated, and the young man soon retired to his room. He did not see how he was to continue living here under such conditions.

The next day he went to see the authorities and showed them his passport.[21] After reading it, the official began to laugh.

"Do you know," he said to the peasants who were present in his office, "we shall have a nobleman in our county. Here he is."

All began to laugh, and the young man said indignantly:

"Why do you laugh? I am not the only one here. Doctor Gostinski, Rudnicki, and Lukovski are all noblemen."

"You are mistaken! They lost their nobility beyond the Urals. You are the only nobleman here!"[22]

"There is another!" someone said.

"Who?"

"Farafantoff."

"Has any one of you seen him?"

"Nobody has seen him, but all laugh at him."

Finally, Mrozovetski himself began to laugh at this democratic country; he laughed at this Siberian peculiarity particularly, shook hands with Andryanek's father, the police official, and went out of the office. Lebiazha, although only a village, had the appearance of a town. The two-story houses, ornamented with carvings, well-made fences, numerous stores, the population more commercial than agricultural, a magnificent orthodox church, and a large saloon—such was the general aspect of the streets. Behind the village, the Tobol, covered with ice, lay among the pine trees, and beyond the river, there was another village, Nagorna. Beyond that again lay the endless white steppe.

Antony climbed a hill and looked about him for a long time. All around was the dead desert and the annihilation of

---

[21] To register his presence as required by the Russian police.

[22] The penalty of internal exile also caused a loss of the status and privileges of the nobility.

Nature; it seemed impossible that any power could give her life. The poor man sighed deeply. He understood the great desire of the others to escape from this dreadful country. He lost all courage and turned toward home apathetically.

The doctor was ready for the journey, and there was a troika of horses ready for Mrozovetski. The old man gave him the necessary instructions and a letter to Shishkin authorizing him to inspect his oxen, and then he set off to purchase the grain.

It was the first time Mrozovetski went on business for his employer, and he disappeared. The doctor returned with the grain, sent it on to the vodka distilleries, and was surprised not to find Antony at home. Shumski had not shown up for a couple of weeks. Miss Marya betrayed neither surprise nor sorrow at the prolonged absence of her fiance. She shrugged her shoulders when her father mentioned it.

"He will be back," she answered indifferently.

"I see you don't care much for him," Mrs. Utovich said indignantly.

"I care as much for him as he cares about my dowry," and she laughed ironically.

"Why did you accept him then?" grumbled her father.

"All men are alike."

"What a heart you have. The Lord preserve everyone from it," said Mrs. Utovich.

"I don't offer it to anyone," the young girl answered sharply.

"Let her be," interrupted the doctor. "She is right. The one who has no heart will be happy, and people will not trample on him. If she is cold, we can't help it! But where is Mrozovetski?"

"Did you give him any money?"

"Do you suspect him already? Antony's friend a thief?" said the old man angrily.

The girl frowned.

"Not at all. He may be honest. I was thinking of robbery. Then again, he might have been taken sick. His clothing isn't good for such cold weather."

"You gave him a coat."

"He returned it. I did not offer it a second time."

"You're prepared to see him freeze?"

"I am glad you are of the same opinion as I," exclaimed Mrs. Utovich triumphantly. "She has no heart."

Even Father Ubish looked at the girl, who leaned over the table and went on with her sewing in silence.

"Though I speak with the tongue of angels but have not charity, I am as sounding brass or a tinkling cymbal," quoted he, in his dead voice.

The doctor was silent awhile, then left the room. As he closed the door, he said to Mrs. Utovich:

"Aunt, put that coat in his room. I will speak to him."

The old woman trotted away to carry out his command. The priest went to the kitchen, from which he had caught the smell of freshly-baked bread. The girl sat sewing. After a moment, tears began to drop on the linen, and she laid aside her work.

From the street came the sound of sleigh bells. She shuddered, rose, and escaped from the room. When Shumski appeared, there was no one in the room. He began to hum. The doctor came down to see him.

"You have forgotten us."

"Not at all. I was deucedly busy."

"Have you seen Mrozovetski?"

"Who is he?"

"Well, my new employee."

"That jackass? No, I haven't seen him."

"I sent him to check up on the oxen. And where do you come from?"

"From Kurhan. Shishkin kept me there the whole week. We took inventory,"

"I can't understand what has become of the boy."

"Perhaps the Kirgiz have robbed him."

"Don't joke. I am seriously anxious about him."

Shumski yawned. He looked tired, and his eyes were red. He rose when Miss Marya entered, but his animation was artificial. His fiancee glanced at him inquisitively and did not throw off her gloomy air. Only Mrs. Utovich laughed at her fiance's jokes.

They finished supper and were seated round the fire talking when the door opened, and Mrozovetski entered. He came in so softly that they did not hear him at first. He was white with cold, and instead of speaking, he only moved his lips. Without taking off his overcoat, he sat down near the fire.

Miss Marya rose and approached him. "Drink," she said, handing him a glass of vodka. "You are frozen to death. Drink quickly."

He swallowed the vodka.

"Judging from your physique, you ought to resist the cold better," exclaimed Shumski. "Today was not very cold. I did not feel it. It is true I am as strong as iron. Miss Marya, why go to so much trouble? This man is not an invalid: he can help himself. Even if I were dying, I would not permit a woman to trouble herself about me like this."

Mrozovetski looked at him in silence.

"Very articulate fellow," muttered Shumski.

"Let him alone; he is cold; he is hardly alive. The one who is to blame for it must serve him now."

Saying this, the doctor looked at his daughter, who was slicing bread. She became very pale; the knife slipped and nicked her hand, drawing blood. The blood dropped on the piece of bread destined for the newcomer, and Mrs. Utovich shouted, "Oh, Lord! Blood on the bread! A bad omen!"

Shumski rushed to get some water, the doctor for some medicine, and Mrs. Utovich for some linen. Mrozovetski looked pitifully with his straightforward glance at the girl.

"You must excuse me," he exclaimed. "I did not come here to take somebody else's bread. I hope I shall not bother you much longer. I see how you hate me."

She tied her handkerchief around her hand and looked at him sharply.

"Nothing personal. It is generally established that I hate everybody," she muttered.

They gathered around her and bandaged her hand, forgetting all about Mrozovetski.

He was already warmer and felt as though he was coming back to life. All at once, he said to the doctor:

"Where do you wish me to put the skins? I brought them with me."

"What skins?"

"The skins of the oxen. I have ten of them, and four are lost, for the dogs scavenged on the carcasses."

"What dogs? What are you talking about?"

"I am talking about the oxen you told me to look after. They had not been taken care of, and the manure stood up to their knees. Fourteen of them dropped dead, and I brought the skins," said Mrozovetski.

"What an agreeable messenger you are," laughed Shumski.

"It was not my duty to take care of them. I am sorry I found them so," answered Mrozovetski calmly.

"I see you have everything in good order," said the doctor turning to Shumski.

"I told you I had been absent for a week. Without me, everything goes wrong. I will teach them a lesson when I get back," replied Shumski.

"You have taught me one already. Fourteen oxen! All earnings lost! But you, where have you been all this week?" the doctor asked, turning to Mrozovetski.

"You must excuse me, but Shishkin detained me in Utyatska."

"What? Shumski tells me that he was with him for a whole week in Kurhan."

"I don't know where Mr. Shumski was, but I know that when I came to Utyatska, Shishkin was in a great deal of trouble. One of his pumps had broken, and he asked me to repair it for him. That took me two days. He told me that when he sees you again, he will apologize to you for my absence."

"Well, well. I see you have found your way into the old bear's goodwill without my protection. I congratulate you on your enterprise."

"I did not use the bear much. I was glad to help a man in his trouble."

"I suppose he paid you well for your work? The old man, when drunk, is very liberal."

"He was sober when I was there."

"Then he was not liberal. Do they appreciate your abilities better in Europe?"

Mrozovetski shrugged and did not reply. He had other bits of news gathered on his journey, but he preferred to keep silent.

The doctor was gloomy and sat pulling at his beard. Shumski was evidently seeking a quarrel. Mrozowicki rose and went to his room.

Only when there did he open his coat and take from his pocket several banknotes. He counted them twice. He had twenty roubles—quite a sum to him in his present state of poverty. Various plans rushed through his head. Although very tired, he could not sleep. His first thought was to go home with this small amount of money and see his fiancee, his sister, and his country. But fear and shame stopped him. Then he thought of buying some clothing, but he regretted parting with the money come by so unexpectedly. The clothing would wear out, and what would he have afterward? Then, his mind half-asleep, his fancy played with splendid business affairs, and he fell asleep dreaming of his estate at Promieniev, which, in his dream, he had succeeded in getting back from the hands of the man who had robbed him.

When he rose the next day, he hid his money and went out. He entered the store and purchased some underclothing and a shirt. He wished to buy some tobacco but decided not to spend the money and resisted the temptation. Then, walking down the street, his thoughts became busy with plans for commencing some business.

"I wish you good health," said someone behind him.

He turned and beheld Andryanek smiling at him.

"Come and see us. This is a holiday. We can then become better acquainted while drinking tea together.

The whole family received the stranger with rough, primitive cordiality. They feasted him on tea and vodka, cedar nuts, and cake. They asked him about his country, about his family, his fiancee, and his business. But they did not envy him for having seen the marvels of civilization.

Andryanek even laughed at them.

"A long summer is dangerous because all kinds of diseases come from the heat. The winter is healthy, and the cold kills off the weaker children so that those who survive are strong like I am," and he stretched his gigantic body.

"What a country!" added his brother with pride.

"Can one become rich here?" asked Mrozovetski.

"Certainly. Have you already started?" asked Andryanek.

"I am employed by the doctor."

"That does not matter. You can go into business just the same. How much money have you got?"

"Almost nothing: twenty roubles."

"It's enough for a start. Will you go into partnership with me?"

"How?"

"We will hire nets and try our luck before the fair."

"Where?"

"In the Tobol. He who has a net will soon have fish if he has good luck. And the work is healthy. Will you do it with me?"

"I will tell you tomorrow. I must first ask my employer."

"All right. When one has no father, his employer must act as his head. Come tomorrow with an axe."

Mrozovetski liked the project; he also liked this great, jolly giant whose eyes shone when there was talk of hunting and hard work with risk attached to it. Andryanek was a healthy and simple-minded representative of a young nation.

Almost decided to go into partnership with his new friend, Mrozovetski went home to get his breakfast, which he ate in the kitchen, not wishing to meet Shumski. The cook's cat was his sole companion. Then he went in to see the doctor. The betrothed couple were talking in the dining room. With great hesitation, he thanked the doctor for his hospitality.

"What? Do you wish to leave us?" asked the old man in astonishment.

"I am an intruder here. No matter how I work, it will always be bad. If I tell you the truth, they will call me an intriguer, and if I am silent, then I will feel that I am not conscientious. It will be better that I go before I disturb your peace."

"This is too quick," said the doctor bitterly. "I thought you would replace my son. I was mistaken."

"No, sir, you were not mistaken; but you already have someone to replace your son."

"Ah, it is true," said the doctor. "My taste does not amount to much here anymore. I must capitulate. I have no right to stop you from going. I am sure Shishkin offered you a position. He is right, and you are right. Here nobody thought even to protect you from the cold. Therefore it is right that you leave me."

He spoke rapidly as though he would like to finish the topic as soon as possible.

"Have you already a position?"

"No, sir."

"Where are you going then?"

"I don't need very much. I will find something."

"Listen. Stay at least until tomorrow. Think it over. Don't act rashly."

"I will stay, but I shall not change my mind," whispered Mrozovetski.

"Well, do as you please. I was mistaken in you."

The young man left the room sad at heart. He felt that he had acted rightly in the matter, yet he was ashamed. It was a pity he could not explain his action to the doctor. The old man was angry. Why? Because Mrozovetski was being discreet.

Mrs. Utovich sent him to the store. He was glad of this. In the evening, they brought him a letter. He trembled, thinking it must be bad news from home. But it was only a proposition from Shishkin to take charge of the distillery. And what about Shumski? He was much astonished.

He was still standing with the letter in his hand, hardly believing his own eyes, when Shumski rushed in. He also held a paper, which he threw on the table.

"You made that denunciation!" he shouted, white with rage.

Mrozovetski took the letter and read it. It contained Shumski's discharge.

"What denunciation are you talking about?" he asked quietly.

"Don't pretend you don't understand. You told him that I gambled in Kurhan."

"Shishkin told me that a rascal and a thief were drinking in Kurhan and that he would chase both of them away. He was drunk then and free with his epithets. I did not know you were connected with the matter. And I care about it no more than I do about last winter's snow. I am not going to take your position, so you have no right to talk to me in that way."

"Why don't you take the position? You hold in your

hand Shishkin's letter, in which he asks you to come."

"The position is not for me. I can't drink vodka and gamble. Don't look around. No one is listening to us. Tomorrow morning I shall leave this house, for I do not wish to be guilty of staying here and keeping anything from them. Shishkin's anger will pass, he will take you back, and you will be on surer footing here. Only don't offend me again because I can also lose my temper."

Shumski turned on his heel and left the room. Mrozovetski ate his supper alone in the kitchen. He was on bad terms with the doctor and with Shumski. He said goodbye to Mrs. Utovich, gave Sergey a few kopeks, and complimented him on his cat. He did not wish to see Miss Marya and decided to depart without taking leave of her.

It was still dark when he rose, made a bundle of his few belongings, and went out. He stopped in the courtyard and took off his cap, having seen Miss Marya coming from the barn.

She stopped and looked at him gloomily.

"I wish to say goodbye and to beg your pardon," he said. "I did not require much and didn't worry you long," and he smiled.

"On the contrary, you have cost me much. You take with you the remainder of the love my father had for me. You stopped long enough to change me from indifference to enmity. It's true the harvest isn't a very good one."

She passed him without further greeting and went into the house.

Mrozovetski was astounded. Because he gave Shumski a chance to get back his position, Shumski hated him. Because he did not wish to cause the girl any trouble, she accused him of robbing her of her father's love. Merciful God, who is guilty here—he or these people? He lost his usual clear judgment, and could only think, in the depths of his soul, that he was very poor, very badly treated, and very sad. Stupid, thrice stupid, *anima vilis*!

CHAPTER IV
The Kurhan Fair

AT length, the long-expected fair at Kurhan came and changed the quiet town into a strange panorama of the Asiatic East. The streets did not afford enough room for business transactions, so the frozen river Tobol was also used. On it were displayed mountains of meat. Skinned and frozen oxen formed whole streets on the ice. Entire sheep, dipped in water and shining with ice, lay piled up in enormous heaps. There were also mounds of cut-up meats, fish, skins, pyramids of butter, barrels of rendered fat—all the riches of the steppe.

Along these peculiar streets passed hundreds and thousands of Siberians: Kirgiz, merchants, agents, carriers, drivers. There was an enormous amount of movement and noise. Further on stood erected sheds with tea, felts, Chinese porcelain, furs, dram shop, and mountains of nuts. Here bargained Chinamen and Southerners, all sorts of strange and wild people, forming a multi-colored mixture of races, clothing, and dialects.

Among this visible merchandise, there also circulated a secret article. Here and there, in a corner, pairs of people could be seen talking secretly. One of them would pull from his large pocket a pair of scales and from the other some small shining grains. These were weighed, and the price agreed upon, then the grains were changed for a large bunch of banknotes. It was stolen gold and very often counterfeit money. Both parties were taking risks.

After sleeping the whole year, Kurhan now held within its bounds many thousands of people, transacting millions of deals.

Already the first day, Mrozovetski sold part of his share of fish, for which he got thirty-five roubles. Shishkin's money brought him good luck, and the misery he had been obliged to undergo had taught him absolute economy. Badly dressed and hungry, he wandered whole days about the fair, looking not for necessities but for things of which he could make use. In the crowd, he met an occasional acquaintance. Old Shishkin stopped him and, having invited him to drink a cup of tea, made him promise that in case there should be any further trouble with his machine, Mrozovetski should help him at least with advice. Then this millionaire in sheepskin overcoat and boots blackened with tar became talkative. He drank one cup of tea after another and, perspiring, told with pleasure the story of his riches.

"I will tell you, my dear friend, how it happened. My father was sentenced to hard labor in Siberia—an old story. He had been branded with a red-hot iron: on one cheek with the letter 'W' and on the other, with the letter 'Z,' and on his forehead, with the letter 'O.' That's also an old story! He married a Siberian woman here in Kurhan. I was a clerk, then a post-driver, then I started a little store, and, afterward, a dram shop. Then I had a salt house and became a gold- miner. Then I began a business on the steppe. I was lucky with that. Then I leased one distillery, and when I got married, my wife brought me another as a dowry; then came a third and fourth, and— suddenly—I was rich. Ho, ho! If the Lord had only given me a son! But only daughters—perfect damnation, my dear boy, and those scoundrels, my sons-in-law, will blow everything when I die. You are a young beginner. Well, have some more tea. For the service you rendered me, I will give you some advice. If you want to be rich, you must remember three things—never say anything about either your profits or your losses; second, don't let the money rest idle; and third, don't disdain any business. I acted that way. Every business is a good business. And you must be honest. Except with the Kirgiz."

Antony, encouraged by the friendliness of the old man, said to him smilingly:

"And what would you do if you had thirty-five roubles in your pocket?"

"Oh, my soul! It is a big capital here! During the fair, you can turn it over a hundred times. If you do not make a hundred roubles during these four days, you are good for nothing. The whole year we work for these four days. Only be careful with gold because you don't know anything about it. When you have tried everything, and have some experience, then you can try gold."

As soon as Shishkin was recognized, he was surrounded by people with different business propositions, and Antony left him. The old man was sincere in his advice because, seeing him go out, he shouted after him:

"Listen, my soul, never risk your whole capital in one transaction—never!"

Again Antony began to wonder what he should begin with. All at once, in the street where the oxen were, some fat merchants called to him:

"Eh, you there! You are doing nothing. Come and help me load the meat."

He hesitated for a second and then, in company with several peasants, began to carry the frozen giants. They received three roubles for helping to load ten wagons. Antony's share was twenty kopeks.

He was standing still, warmed with the work, when he heard Shumski's familiar laugh. He was walking with Miss

Marya toward the porcelain store. Antony had already grown so wise that he did not blush but only bowed silently.

"Whom do I see? You, student of technology, carrying dead animals?" exclaimed Shumski. "I suppose your time is not very expensive. Can I buy it?"

"What for?" asked Antony.

"Carry a letter for me to Smolin. He is waiting for me at the club, but I don't care to see him now."

Antony smiled,

"I will carry the letter for fifteen kopeks," he said, "because the club is on my way."

Shumski looked at him hesitatingly, astonished. Finally, he gave him the letter and money.

"Oh, *anima vilis*!" he said, in a low voice to Miss Marya. Then added aloud:

"You could have asked me to pay you more for this pleasure."

"When my time is more valuable, your pleasure will cost you more," answered Antony, going away.

At the club, they were drinking and playing cards. Before the gambler Smolin lay a pile of money. He was drunk and feverish. He swore after reading the letter from his gay comrade but continued to play. The room was dark with smoke and the fumes of alcohol. Mrozovetski left the club with relief and, at a spot near the club, purchased from a peasant three barrels of cedar nuts. They were selling well to passers-by in retail, but the peasant was in a hurry, and after a little bargaining, Antony took his place and began to sell it to children and grown-ups by the handful. Andryanek found him at this occupation. Dressed in his best clothes, the young man was taking a pleasure stroll with two gigantic girls, thick as barrels, homely, red, each weighing two hundred pounds. He treated these beauties to nuts purchased from his friend and chatted with him for a while.

"Have you seen the shaman yet?" he asked.

"Who is he?"

"He sits over there in that shanty. He will tell you your
fortune, pull out your teeth, and sell you medicine. Who knows
who he is? He is always at the fair. They say he also sells gold,
but one must be careful in dealing with him, for he can cheat the
smartest of us. He can tell everything from cards. I am going to
see him. It costs only five kopeks."

He took his tall girls and went away.

From his place, Antony could see the whole square. Not
far from him, Doctor Gostinski had scales, and the tradesmen
were selling him butter in enormous quantities. The old man
himself sat the whole day at the scales, having no one to take his
place. He looked tired and cold.

Towards evening, after Antony had sold out all his
merchandise, and without stopping to count up his profits, he
rushed over to the doctor. He pitied the old man.

"Can I help you?" he asked, greeting him. "You must be
tired. Go and rest."

"Ah, it's you. I am glad you came. I am frozen to the
bone. Shumski promised to come at noon and take my place,
but it all ended in a promise. May God reward you for your help.
Here is the money. Take care of the scales. I am going to the·bar-
room to warm up a little."

He remained for a few minutes with Mrozovetski and
then left him alone.

Antony began to receive and weigh the merchandise. On
one occasion, he was slow in dealing with a tradesman who said
he was in a great hurry. Antony paid no attention to his repeated
requests to make haste. He apparently busied himself with the
weights and with looking for a match to light his cigarette, but,
in the meanwhile, he maintained a constant lookout for
someone. At length, he perceived Andryanek coming out of the
fortune-teller's booth and called him.

The peasant approached swiftly.

"What is the matter?" he asked.

"Be my witness while I call a policeman. There are stones

66

in the butter."

"Ah, you rascal," shouted Andryanek, shaking his fist threateningly at the tradesman.

Hearing the shouting, the crowd soon surrounded the shed. The man, seeing that he was in a tight place, jumped into his sleigh, snapped the reins over the horses' necks, and escaped, shoving passers-by aside.

He left his butter behind, and after they had removed the stones, there remained six puds (over 200 hundred pounds) of pure butter. Antony rejoiced, and Andryanek rushed to tell the good news to the doctor.

The doctor came immediately and gave half the butter the trader had abandoned to Antony.

"Take it. It's yours," he said.

At once, Antony's joy forsook him; he blushed and stood looking at the butter.

"Don't worry about it," said the old man, "I will change it into money for you. You need not carry it about. It is worth twenty roubles."

"He had good luck!" exclaimed someone in the crowd.

Antony took his reward without thanks, and not wishing to be the subject of looks and remarks, he squeezed through the crowd and disappeared. The doctor looked after him, wondering what the matter was.

"Is he not satisfied?" thought he. "A grasping fellow. Well, I did not suspect him of that until now."

Antony strolled about for a long time until he succeeded in overcoming his inexpressible grief at being thus misunderstood. He followed the crowd and finally, at nightfall, entered an inn. He ate a scanty supper and afterward, while resting on a bench, swore never to render anyone another service. When he again entered the square, he thought only of his capital and made plans for further business. The coming of the night did not stop the trading. On account of the snow and the Aurora Borealis, it was almost as bright as day. The crowd circulated without rest. Everybody was in feverish haste.

"Haven't you a carriage? I need one." Antony heard on every side.

He liked the idea of having a horse and wagon, but he thought it best to wait until spring. In the meantime, his shoulders served him to carry heavy weights, and he hastened about perspiring, notwithstanding the cold, and gathering in silver and copper money. He kept repeating to himself Shishkin's statement that he should have a hundred roubles at the close of the fair. Toward morning, tired to death, he passed an inn, where a great crowd of people came to have their fortunes told and to purchase patent medicine. A sign, in rough letters, described the shaman's great powers and offered his services to the public. Antony followed the others and entered the shed.

From the first room, where they were selling tea and snacks, the people passed further in, paying the fee—five kopeks—to a woman who sat at the door. Antony paid also and entered a long narrow room where there were only a table, a wooden trunk, and a stove, with a man sitting near it. The man was dressed in a long *khalat*,[23] and a very high, peaked felt cap with fur fringe, like a Kirgiz. His complexion was dark, and his uncombed hair and beard gave him a wild appearance. He turned his piercing eyes and hawk-like nose toward his newest client. He looked like a hideous spider lying in wait for its prey. Antony looked at him, and was seized with fright and repulsion as if beholding a snake. Mechanically, he retreated toward the door, but it was closed, and he soon became ashamed of being so feeble-minded.

In the meanwhile, the sorcerer rose noiselessly and, walking like a spirit, approached Mrozovetski. He squinted his eyes and moved his jaws as though he were chewing. Under the influence of this gaze, Antony felt as though he were paralyzed;

---

[23] A long overcoat adopted from the common Jewish dress

68

he stood waiting in silence. This lasted for some time. It seemed to him as if those eyes entered his soul, piercing his whole being.

Finally, the shaman spoke. He had a harsh voice with a decidedly foreign accent.

"What is your name?"

Antony started and said with difficulty:

"I am a stranger. You don't know me."

"It is exactly because you are a stranger that I ask your name. And perhaps I do know you. What do you wish?"

"You are foretelling fortunes; tell me mine."

The shaman pulled cards from his coat and began to lay them on the table. His hands trembled, and he constantly looked at the young man.

"Are your parents still living?" he asked.

"No."

"A sister?"

"Yes."

"Do you wish to know what has been or what will be?"

By this time, Antony had calmed down.

"Can you tell me if I shall be successful here?"

"Yes, you will be successful, but not easily and not soon. There will be a death—then, sickness and losses. You will succeed if a certain man helps you. Search for him! Search!"

Antony looked at the cards.

"Shall I find him?"

"Yes, but it will cost you much. You must first gather much money. Your foes are very powerful."

"How far off is the man who will help me?"

"No place on earth is ever far. Search!"

"You mentioned a death. Who will die?"

"Your sweetheart. It will be a heavy blow. Have you been long in this country?"

"Not very."

"Then you are not yet devoured by homesickness. Aha! And there, in your country, how is it? Misery?"

Antony only nodded.

Again the shaman looked at him inquisitively. He asked him some short and indifferent questions as though wishing to gather material for his predictions. But Mrozovetski would not speak much about himself. The sorcerer had guessed something, but he could not say what.

The young man put his hand in his pocket and said:
"How much?"

The shaman began to tremble.

"A rouble. A silver rouble. You will give me a hundred when my prediction is realized. Don't you need medicine? It doesn't cost much! And perhaps you will buy some gold? Here it is!"

He took out a dirty little bag and poured from it some different-sized grains, which he immediately gathered together with his hooked fingers. Antony was again seized with an aversion for the man's spider-like movements. He threw a rouble on the table and retreated toward the door.

"Be in good health! I wish you success," said the sorcerer. "I shall see you next year."

"I don't think so," answered the young man, going out. He was angry with himself for having made this visit to the sorcerer. He was trying to get away from the place without being noticed when he met Andryanek, who, a little tipsy now, singing and shouting, was driving his wild troika through the crowd.

"Climb up!" he called to his fishing companion. "I have no more business here. I have bought all that I had to buy and blown all the rest. The shaman predicted a wedding for me. Let us go home. No one decent is left at the fair."

This invitation pleased Antony, and he jumped into the sleigh, and they galloped off.

"Well, and what did the shaman predict for you?"
"Nonsense!"
"How much did you pay him?"
"One rouble."

"Smart! He knows how to shave a customer! I gave him twenty kopeks."

"Then he cheated me twice over. I deserve it for my stupidity."

"And how much did you make on the fair?"

"I haven't counted yet."

"And what are you going to do now?"

"I shall buy a horse and a wagon."

"Good idea! I will sell you my mare, cheap. I now have a younger one."

"Will you feed her through the winter?"

"I will. I have plenty of hay, and she will work for her oats. You had better stay with us. We will drive round together until you learn the business."

"Very well. I will live with you, and for your help, I shall be most grateful."

"Don't mention it. I like you. You shall play for me at my wedding."

"Andryanek, you are a good fellow! "

"And you are a good companion. Here we are in Lebiazha."

Antony slipped his hand in his pocket and felt his money with delight. At last, he felt solid ground beneath his feet, and joy entered his heart.

CHAPTER V
You Must Die in Order to Live

A WEEK after the fair, Miss Marya was obliged to inspect her dram shops. None of their horses was available, as the doctor had gone to Shchedrynsk to purchase more rye. She, therefore, sent to Kvasnikoffs'—this was Andryanek's name—to get a sleigh.

After some time, the sleigh bells resounded in front of the house, and a little later, Mrozovetski entered the kitchen, whip in hand.

Mrs. Utovich clapped her hands.

"What, a guest! Sit down! Sit down! I shall not let you go until Marya gets back. I will feel lonely. We will talk about our country."

"I did not come on a visit. Andryanek is away. Maybe, Miss Marya will hire my horse and sleigh. I have a good horse."

"Ah, it's true! You are now a coachman," said Miss Marya with a smile. "Very well. Let us be going."

They looked at him carefully, and Mrs. Utovich said:

"You are not looking well. Are you sick? Ah, yes, you had a letter from Europe. It was delivered here. My Lord! Perhaps it contained some·bad news from your sweetheart? She must be longing for you."

The boy blushed.

"Well, that cannot be helped," he answered, turning his head away.

Miss Marya began to dress for the journey, and the old woman prattled on:

"You should have brought her with you. It's difficult to bear love in separation. Have you written to her?"

"Quite a long time ago. I don't have much time, and then there's nothing to write."

"Well, send her a kiss, at least! Mr. Shumski writes every week and sometimes twice a week."

"Let us be going," said Miss Marya. "But where is Sergey?"

"Where? In the dram shop, to be sure! My dearest, don't leave me alone. This drunkard will freeze outside. My dear Mr. Antony, have pity! Go and bring him inside. What can I do with that frozen log? I can't bring him in from the snow if he falls."

"I will bring him in right away," said Antony, leaving the room.

He brought the "log" and put "it" in the kitchen. Sergey protested that he was sober and summoned Katalay as his witness. He promised to get the dinner ready, but he could move neither hand nor foot. Mrs. Utovich began to scold him, and in the meanwhile, the young people went out.

Mrozovetski's horse and sleigh were very decent, and the old mare was well kept—Miss Marya noticed this immediately. Antony wrapped up her feet carefully, patted the dog, Tomoy, and they were off.

It was still dreadfully cold. They had not spoken a word since their farewell, and their last conversation at the time when Antony left the house was in the mind of each, and it made them both uneasy.

They stopped before the first dram shop in Petrofka. The bar-tender recognized Antony and greeted him.

"Glory to God! You are already in business?" he said, handing Mrozovetski a glass of vodka.

Antony smiled. He sat with downcast eyes, caressing the dog. He awakened, as from a dream, when Miss Marya called him.

"Have a shot of vodka?" she said.

"No, thank you."

On their way home, she said:

"It's strange how this dog likes you, although generally, he does not like strangers."

"Dogs sometimes recognize a friendly soul better than human beings."

"Then my dog has no chance to show his talents."

"If you say so," he answered. She noticed that this had hurt him.

"You have a good horse. Did you do well during the fair?"

"Counting your father's present, I earned one hundred roubles. I shall be able to live on that until spring. But here, the spring comes very late."

"The snow will disappear in May, but we have no real spring here. All at once, without any transition, the short, burning summer follows the cold weather. Then in October, winter commences again. We who must live here never see any spring."

Antony dropped the reins and turned toward her. A light passed over his face.

"In our spring," he said, breathing in deeply, "even though it may be grey and, like the winter, without any bright coloring, how much life and health there is in it. It is February now, and in our country, toward noon, the sun is bright, and the wind is heavy. Hope then springs in the heart."

Miss Marya shook her head.

"Mr. Mrozovetski," she said. "You must not speak of it. Here one must not speak of those things. You don't know yet how careful one must be here, even with his thoughts. It is all poison, and it paralyzes both the will and the thought."

74

"Then you also know all about it?" he said, sighing.

She smiled sadly.

"I was three years old when my parents came here. My brother was eight. Twenty years ago! I spent seventeen years in Kurhan. There I have become accustomed to being... a Siberian. I know, also, that I shall die here. Therefore I am forbidden to think of my country."

"Then you never long to get away?" he asked, seeing no indiscretion in questioning her.

"I never said anything about it to anyone," she said thoughtfully, "but it seems to me that I have finally overcome that longing. But that has made me wicked. I think that a person who is forbidden to love his own country cannot love anything. Such a man or woman does not attain his full development—he does not blossom but becomes dried-up like stubble."

Antony listened, astonished. Then she was interested in something other than business and accounts?

"Then you also know this longing?" he asked again.

"I was once young, you know. I saw three such springs as you speak of. For three years, I was in a boarding school in Warsaw. I was meant to remain there, but my mother became ill, and I returned to take care of her. She was ill for a long time, and I was obliged to keep the house and look after the store and the dram shops. To stifle my longing, I worked at the accounts at night. Then I fell very, very ill myself. And my mother died. I remained here. I recovered. This snow is mine, you see. This house is mine. This sun is mine. This country yields riches, health, and liberty. It's a paradise compared with that other."

She laughed bitterly, and her dark eyes grew darker and more gloomy.

Mrozovetski shivered.

"As for me, if I can only last until spring, I shall go back," murmured he. "I will go to my poor country on foot if I must."

"Because there you have someone for whom you care."

"If I really cared for them, I should stay here. You

yourself said that this country yields riches and freedom. But in my misery, I do not think of these things. Do you know? There are some days when one is afraid to touch a knife. Some nights when one groans like a tortured spirit. It is hard to get through twenty-four hours of that. How then could one bear a whole lifetime of it?"

"Others have suffered the same—and lived," she said.

"If I were not ashamed of myself, and if it were not out of pity for my sister, I should have killed myself long ago. I suppose others must be stronger than me. Perhaps you needn't have rescued me that night. I can't stand it. I can't. I shall go back."

"Or you will be cured and become... a machine without feeling! You have too much time to think."

"I can do nothing. For two weeks, I have not been able to sleep. I cannot eat. Perhaps I am losing my mind."

"Like Father Ubish."

"I sometimes wonder if I shall live until spring."

She looked at him, as one might look at a child, and began to speak softly.

"In the beginning, it is only an indescribable sadness and uneasiness. One cannot work or give attention to anything. Then comes internal rebellion and hatred of the people and anger toward even inanimate objects. Then the mad desire to run, or die, as the only means of salvation."

"It is as though you read my thoughts."

"It is the Siberian sickness, as my father says. Then comes the crisis: a listlessness, an indifference to the environment, and to the impressions of the senses. It seems that the soul leaves the body and seeks its own country, for to one's ears seem to come sounds from far away, and to his nostrils faint scents, and before one's eyes rise views which are not of this country. By then, one has become wicked but is yet harmless. But when the spirit returns, it brings with it the instinct to move, to survive and one forgets the past. One no loger mentions it, no longer thinks of

76

it, but it is the end of youth, of joy, of sentiment, of his better self. He becomes just like the people born here. Have you not noticed that they never laugh heartily? They are never merry without vodka! This country stunts the human mind; the people are all feelingless machines."

"I do not wonder that Zdanowski became a drunkard and that Rudnicki wishes to marry a Siberian girl. Despair urges them on to excesses. I am afraid for myself."

"Why do you not bring your fiancee here? I suppose it is easier to suffer when one is not alone."

"She is not well. My sister writes me that she is coughing. Such is my lot!"

They arrived at the second dram shop, and the conversation stopped. It was now noon, and she invited Mrozovetski to dine with her.

He refused, but she insisted cordially, talking to him as to a sick man.

"If you do not eat, you will lose strength and will be unable to survive until spring. And if you become ill, how will you be able to earn money for your return journey? You must eat. You must shake off this apathy."

She touched his shoulder, handing him some meat. He looked at her with very sad eyes and obeyed like a child. He ate and drank. She then assigned him to count the cash in order to prevent him from sinking back into apathy while she looked over the book accounts. As he worked, he became more cheerful, looked at the people, and attended to his horse. She tried every means to keep him from thinking of the dangerous topic, and when they reached the third dram shop, she began to instill other thoughts into his mind.

"It's not enough that you should be a mere driver," she said. "You must find some other occupation. Shishkin asks my father for you every time they meet. Why did you not accept the position he offered you?"

"I do not wish to be in anyone's way—especially yours."

"You mean Shumski's? You would only render him a service. Once his large and easily earned salary is cut off, he would become more serious and stop his spendthrift ways. He has too good a position, and I fear this prosperity will turn his mind. And then, Shumski is a cosmopolitan. He will make a career anywhere. He is a lawyer by profession, a merchant by inclination, and a mechanical engineer by accident."

Antony smiled.

"Grand education, that, not like me, *anima vilis*," he murmured.

"Were you angry with him?"

"I? With Shumski? I should then be very stupid, even more stupid than he imagines me."

"I was sure that you did not care what he said."

"It's a common thing in the world. A man who is poor, alone, and humiliated—he is an *anima vilis* for the amusement of his fellow-men. In Siberia, as well as in Europe, the same principle applies."

He whipped up his horse and added with a smile:

"I am accustomed to it. Fate and mankind have tested me. My life was hard, and my sister, observing it, used to say, 'Antony, you deserve happiness. Fate is your debtor, and one day she will pay you.'"

Miss Marya made an impatient movement, and her eyes again became dark.

"That is not true," she said bitterly. "Man's luck is for life. One is born to enjoy life, to succeed in love, in winning general favor, or to use others. Another is born to be hated, treated with indifference, or forgotten altogether. A man who is not born with good luck gets no pay for his suffering."

"That is not true," he said with gentle dignity. "Honest work brings its own peace, and poverty borne patiently makes a man better-natured and more open. Perhaps he who has the least for himself has the most in himself. That also constitutes riches."

"Then you do not rebel?" she asked, curious to hear his reply.

"Never. I cannot rebel against my fate because I have never been well off. I have always been poor, insignificant, and downtrodden. Always. Some of my fellow creatures have laughed at me, others have abused me; no one has loved me but your brother, and he is no more. Therefore I can be satisfied with anything and suffer much, and I think, even if fate does not repay me, I shall not sin against my fellows who are more fortunate than I. It serves one's honor and self-respect."

Miss Marya dropped her head and bit her lips.

"You are a piece of perfection!" she said in her usual icy voice.

He was surprised at this sudden change and looked at her in astonishment.

"Have I offended you in any way?" he asked gently. "If I have, you must pardon me."

"No! You have had the opportunity to see me and judge me as others have. I don't consider myself any better than that."

He did not understand, but her face bore such a repellent look that he dared not question her. After a while, he asked timidly:

"Do you permit your driver to smoke?"

"Certainly."

"We must take the dog in the sleigh. The poor thing is exhausted. Jump in, Tomoy!"

He noticed that Marya's feet were not well covered, so he stopped and wrapped them up carefully.

"It is not at all necessary. I am very well as I am."

"We still have ten versts to drive. Are you not cold?"

His dark brown eyes had in them that same calm goodness and quiet, which were the essence of his being. And his soul seemed like a piece of refined gold, cleansed of its baser alloy in the fire of adversity and misfortune. He did not understand her sudden fancies and bitter outbursts, but he knew now how to treat her, the ice of diffidence being broken·between them.

"Perhaps you would be willing to employ me more often? If Doctor Gostinski is likely to be late, I can go tomorrow and fetch the vodka."

"Yes! It's easier than to live under the same roof with us," she answered sharply.

"Well, I couldn't stand it," he said frankly.

"My father was very upset when you left."

"It would have been worse had I remained. I am not a very gay companion, and I should only have been in the way."

"Yes, you did not wish to expose yourself to annoyance. It was more comfortable to retreat and not have your peace disturbed."

"I did not wish to repay you with ingratitude for saving my life."

"Then you believe that to keep one in ignorance of a falsehood is a service and a proof of gratitude? I can assure you then that I am not ignorant, and I call your decision an act of cowardice and ingratitude. If my father knew, he would be even more resentful than he is now when he thinks you left only on account of egotism and greed."

"You are perfectly right, but I could not act differently."

"Yes. You are freer now. It is better to be independent in a peasant's hut than to serve in a mansion. But, at any rate, you should come and see us. My father would be much pleased. The evenings are long. What do you do when you do not drive?"

"I assist my friends. With Andryanek, I knit fish nets, I build furniture, I fetch wood. I did not come to see you because you bade me goodbye in such a manner that I understood I was not to trouble you anymore."

"Ought I to apologize?"

"Not at all. I must have been guilty if you were angry. But if you permit it, I will come next Sunday to serve at mass."

"Very well. Rogovski has gone to Tobolsk."

80

In the distance, the onion dome of the orthodox church emerged, and soon they reached home.

"Will you come in so that I can pay you?"

"No matter. Leave it until I have earned more. Then I shall have some credit in your store."

"Then come tomorrow to collect the vodka you will take to our shops."

"I will be here at daybreak."

He saluted and drove away.

The next day he came as promised and went on to deliver vodka to the dram shops. When he got back, the doctor was at home, and they made him stay for the evening. The old man was evidently fond of him and inquired solicitously regarding his projects and means, giving him some good advice. He also inquired what news he had had from the old country.

Antony did not tell him of his plans and tried to conceal the fact that he was very low-spirited. After that, he did not put in an appearance for several days, as they did not ask him. Neither did he come on Sunday. They saw nothing more of him.

"He is out of sorts again," the doctor said to himself.

One day, old Marcyanna, the mother of one of the Polish settlers, came to the store and said:

"Do you know, Miss Marya, that the young man who lived with you for a while is dying?"

"Impossible!" exclaimed the girl.

"Seems impossible, but true! I was there yesterday. There was a wedding at Kvasnikoffs', and they invited me. Andryanek himself said to me: 'I am glad I have a wife now, but I am also sorrowful for my friend. Antony is dying.'

"I went to see him. He didn't recognize me, but I told him that I was his countrywoman and had come to help him. He asked me to bring him a priest. Perhaps Father Ubish could see him. He is one of us, and he deserves it."

Miss Marya listened quietly. Then she locked the store

and went to see her father. The old man was shocked and worried. He would not wait for breakfast but went immediately to see the young man.

When he returned, Mrs. Utovich ran out to greet him.

"Is he dead?" she asked.

"No. He caught a cold and is devoured by the Siberian fever. I will save him from the fever, but I cannot cure his sadness. Somebody should have looked after him. The people with whom he lives are good souls, but they don't understand his needs."

"I am going to him to read him some prayers," said Mrs. Utovich, and she wrapped herself in her shawl and took her worn-out prayer book. In order to be prepared for anything, she also took a blessed candle and a bottle of holy water.

Antony had a little room behind the kitchen. The air was damp and thick. He had furnished the room himself and stored there all his wealth: the harness and oats for the mare, parts of a wagon made by himself, a few sheepskins bought off the Kirgiz, an old felt blanket, a hatchet, a tin samovar, and several other small articles, all jumbled together without any attempt at order. He sat all day long on a straw mattress near the stove. In that position, the old woman found him, and she sensed that he must soon die.

She wished to talk, but he did not answer, so she sat at the window and began to read from her book, one prayer after another, looking from time to time to see if she should light the candle. The daylight faded, the old woman grew hoarse, and the sick man drew nearer the stove, shaking spasmodically and groaning pitifully. Mrs. Utovich lighted the candle.

At that moment, someone softly opened the door, and Miss Marya appeared on the threshold.

"What are you doing?" she asked, frightened.

"Well, he is dying."

"Has he taken his medicine?"

"There is no need to trouble him with medicine. Don't

you see he is dying? Perhaps Father Ubish could give him absolution.”

The girl looked at the sick man, touched his forehead and hands, and then, without saying anything, blew out the candle and lighted an oil lamp. Then she called Andryanek.

“Haven’t you another room?”

“We do, but he didn’t want it.”

“He can’t oppose us now. We must take him out of here.”

The peasant took Antony in his arms and carried him to another room: Andryanek’s parents gave him their own. The women followed.

They put him to bed, and Miss Marya forced him to take some medicine. Then she mixed a hot drink, recommended Andryanek to watch over him until the next morning, drew the curtains, and went away. Mrs. Utovich trotted after her, her religious sentiments much outraged, and repeating angrily:

“You will see! It will be as I said. You will see!”

“We shall see!” retorted the girl.

But the next day, Antony was still alive.

“You would have burned the whole candle for nothing,” said Marya jokingly.

“Well, he is young and strong, so his soul leaves the body slowly. He may live a couple of days longer.”

The doctor went again to see him and came back looking very grave. He prepared a new tincture and said to his daughter:

“Take this to him. I don’t know that I can pull him through. He has the same symptoms as Antony.”

Without displaying any emotion, the girl took the medicine and went out.

This time, Antony recognized her.

“You must excuse me,” he whispered. “There is no need to trouble yourself like this. I thank you, but I doubt I will be able to repay you. Except maybe that I will take your greetings to Antony.”

He spoke quietly and without regret.

"I was preparing for my journey, but I see that I must stay here a little longer. I should like to write to my sister, but I can't move. Well, she will soon know just the same."

"I will write whatever you wish, but there is no need. You will soon be well again. Take your medicine, please."

"It is no use wasting the medicine. Why should I get better? One must die some day. I am glad I shall have some rest soon."

"I didn't know you were such a lazy man," she said, giving him his medicine. "Not he who wishes will die, but he who does not wish it—and when he does not wish it."

"You must not deprive me of hope," he smiled wanly. "If you would be so kind... would you write a letter to my sister? I will dictate it."

She found a sheet of paper, and he, looking into space, began softly:

"Dear Valka:

"I was robbed to the bone in Tobolsk, and from there, things went badly: you know my luck. After arriving here, I managed to make enough money to buy a horse and a sleigh, but what would I get out of it?—a piece of daily bread! I would be of no use or consolation to you. The frosts are terrible here, and I didn't have good clothes, so I came down with a fever. And now it looks like it is over with me.

"And let me tell you one more thing. I was only looking for spring to escape this place. I couldn't stand it here. So either I would have gotten lost somewhere along the way home, or I would have lost my health and only arrived home penniless and caused you trouble, so this is better. I have saved enough to pay for my burial. My neighbors will bury me, and I will lie quietly next to Antoś Gostyński. I am sorry to send such bad news, but it is better that you should know the truth immediately than be kept in uncertainty. I am bidding you farewell.

"Be careful how you tell Jozia about it. Thank her for her

84

kindness, and take care of her for my sake. If I have caused you sorrow, pardon me and remember me in your prayers. I am very weak. I will ask to have the date of my death written in this letter, so you will know when I ceased thinking of you. It is very, very cold here. And very empty."

Miss Marya stopped writing and looked sadly at the letter. The sick man, completely exhausted, lay quiet. She folded the letter and stood motionless for a while. Her own troubles seemed petty and small when she compared them with the bitterness of this man's fate. Poor, sick, alone, after a hard life, after a continuous fight with adverse fortune, he was now leaving the world without any protest, without complaint. He had had no pleasure, but he had not whined. She felt an intense pity for him. She approached the bed softly and gave him something to drink. She thought of the many times she had offended him and felt guilty and humiliated.

A noise was heard in the house, and Mrs. Utovich rushed in.

"Marya! What a misfortune! Shumski has arrived," she said, out of breath.

"What of it? Father is at home."

"No, he isn't. I told Shumski that you had gone to see the Kotnitskis. He waited for an hour and then wanted to go after you. I was dreadfully frightened and ran all the way here myself. Jesus! If he finds out!"

"If he finds out what?" the girl asked impatiently.

"That you are here with an unmarried man!"

Antony, awakened by the conversation, opened his eyes and listened.

"Are you out of your mind?" asked Miss Marya. "Please go and tell him the truth and entertain him until I return."

" It's you who are out of your mind!" said the angry old woman. "Is he your brother that you are looking after him? Your father told you to do it, but you should have disobeyed your father. He doesn't know what is proper. There is no common sense in risking your reputation for the sake of a stranger. It is not the place for a young girl.”

“That is true,” whispered Antony. “Yet again, I cause you trouble. Pray, forgive me. I thank you for everything you have done. And now goodbye. We shall not see each other again. May God give you all happiness.”

Mrs, Utovich was suddenly ashamed of her outburst and became silent.

Miss Marya was pale, and her eyes shone. She prepared to go without visible haste.

“I will come again toward evening,” she said. “You must not think of dying. Don’t forget to take your medicine. My father will be here within an hour. I will send some broth and some milk. I am sure you will be better soon.”

The women did not speak on the way home.

Shumski met them halfway. He was very cross.

“Where do you come from?” he asked stiffly, looking at his watch.

“I visited a sick man,” she answered coolly.

“I was told that you had gone to see the Kotnitskis.”

“Aunt thought I had gone there: I am not accustomed to report to her or anyone else where I go.”

Shumski bit his lips. They entered the house, and Miss Marya went to the kitchen.

“Grinya!” she called. “Take some broth and milk, and take it to Andryanek for Mr. Mrozovetski.”

The old woman trembled, and Shumski smiled bitterly.

“Then Mr. Mrozovetski is the object of your special and solicitous attentions?”

“Yes.”

Mrs. Utovich tried to intervene.

“The poor thing is dying,” she said. “The doctor says he is liable to die at any moment.”

“Not a great loss,” growled Shumski.

Miss Marya went upstairs, and Shumski followed her. In

86

the dining room, he stopped her.

"My queen, permit me to kiss your hands. I haven't seen you for such a long time."

She offered him her hand but remained indifferent and distracted.

"I hurried to you with good news," he continued, looking tenderly into her eyes. "I have received a letter from my parents giving their consent to our marriage. My father presents me with a drug store in Suwalki, and he awaits us impatiently. There is nothing now in the way of our happiness, and I beseech you to appoint the day for our wedding. I am dying of impatience. Be merciful to your most humble servant."

He drew her nearer and embraced her, but she drew back hastily and with determination.

"You know that I am not fond of tender scenes. I am glad you have your parents' consent, but I do not wish to be married before my time of mourning is over. I shall observe it for my father's sake, if nothing else. My brother's death is too recent for me to think of marrying now. And why should we hasten? Your contract only ends in two years."

"Just enough time to sell up."

"Sell up what?"

"You. I have only the capital. I am speaking of your father's business here."

"My father has no intention of selling up. That was his condition. He has told you that. If you stay here, you will get everything. If not, if you take me away, you take me with five thousand roubles dowry. That has not changed."·

"Yes, I know it, but I thought that when your father got to know me better, he would change his mind and come with us."

"I don't believe he would."

"But we cannot leave him alone. In case he should die, these people here would steal everything before we could return to collect it."

Miss Marya began to laugh.

"Well, then, you go alone, and I will remain here to look after the business," she said.

Shumski blushed.

"You misunderstood me. If your father made me his superintendent, I would arrange everything. He is of venerable age, and it is time he took rest. I will sacrifice my inclinations and undertake the work. Perhaps later, we can persuade him to go with us."

"The money does not concern me at all. Speak to my father about it."

"But you will help me, will you not?"

"I have no influence over my father. Notwithstanding his age, he has a will of his own. If he consents, I will not oppose it."

"You have no heart. I get nothing in exchange for my love," he complained.

"You received what you asked for: my hand. You have known me for two years, and it seems that I am the same always."

"Yes, the same always—pitiless and cruel."

She shrugged her shoulders.

"I am the same to everybody," she answered bitterly.

Mrs. Utovich looked in, but, seeing the two seated near each other, she relaxed. She began to lay the table, glancing at them from time to time. She was glad that everything was all right.

Shumski remained all day and was then obliged to stay overnight for a heavy snowstorm set in on the steppe. They spoke of business and the approach of spring. In the meantime, a high wind shrieked round about the house, and the snow fell thickly, cutting off all communication with the outside world.

Miss Marya bent over her sewing with her thoughts on Mrozovetski. It was impossible to go to him, and perhaps the poor boy was in agony.

The next day, and the day after, no one was able to go to see him. The great snowstorm continued, and all of Lebiazha was buried. There was no pathway even to the barns, and the village showed no signs of life.

Shumski still remained, wearied but trying not to show it and speaking with uneasiness about the distilleries, saying he'd have to get back to work as soon as he could.

Finally, on the fourth day, a great cold descended—forty below—and the storm quieted. The people began to move about again. First, Shumski went away, and then Marya, as usual, went to visit the dram shops. She sent to inquire about Mrozovetski. He was alive, so the doctor immediately went to see him. And Marya put away the letter she had written to his sister and was glad the poor boy lived.

Then she became absorbed in her work, and only once her father mentioned him to her.

"He is stronger than Antony," he said as though he regretted it.

At last, Mrozovetski was on his feet again and came to thank them for their care. He placed ten roubles before the doctor.

"What do you mean?" asked the old man with great indignation. "Do you mean to pay me?"

"Yes. The medicine was an expense to you, and the wine and broth also. When I caught the thief, it did not cost me anything, and you paid me for it. If you estimate a service at a price, I must be permitted to do the same, even if I am poorer than you."

"I didn't know you were so sensitive. At that time, I thought you were not satisfied because I had not paid you enough. Well, put your money in your pocket, and forgive me this time. You are not rich enough to pay me for the joy I have in seeing you alive. If you wish to pay your debt, come to see me more often when you have time."

Seeing that the boy hesitated, he took the bill and put it

into his pocket, and then embraced him.

At that moment, Tomoy jumped on him with a cordial greeting. Behind the dog, Miss Marya appeared.

"Hello," she said with a smile, shaking hands with him.

Mrs. Utovich also came to congratulate him, and even Sergey smiled a greeting. Everybody was glad to see him alive. He spent the evening with them, and the doctor was cheerful in his company. The young girl also talked more than usual. They even laughed a little when he told them about Andryanek's wedding and the mistakes made by the new groom. He related the village gossip to Mrs. Utovich, and she was so delighted that she offered to read his future form cards. Then he told them of his visit to the shaman.

"Oh, he is a trickster!" said the doctor. "He is not a shaman at all. He lives out on the steppe about three hundred miles from here. He owns a farm there. I used to visit him when I went around selling scythes. He built a small fortress of dirt and wood. He must be rich, for he deals in gold and counterfeit banknotes. I have known him for twenty years. They say he has escaped from a forced labor camp. I see him every year at the fair."

Mrozovetski only half listened, for, in the meantime, Mrs. Utovich was telling him marvelous things with the cards. It was quite late when he wished them good night, and Miss Marya said:

"Stay until tomorrow. You are not yet strong. You could relapse very easily. That room is still empty, you know.

"Thank you, but I must return and feed my horse."

"That is true. You have your duties," she laughed.

"I make my living from the beast. I must take care of her," he said.

The doctor urged him to come again.

The next day, Antony counted his money and then asked Andryanek's advice.

Acting on this, he purchased an old rifle, and

thenceforth, when he was not busy driving, he went out on the steppe, at first with a friend and then alone, once he was better acquainted with the country. He became a very enthusiastic huntsman, and the vast solitude of the profession suited his mood.

After a month of understudy, he began to set out at every opportunity along the shores of the river Tobol or through the birch wood half-covered with snow, and sometimes when he went too far, it was late at night before he reached home.

The fatigue and hard work helped him to conquer his sadness, and he preferred to go out on the steppe than to go driving because, with the gliding motion of the sleigh, sad thoughts came trooping back.

Andryanek was a faithful friend. He made him familiar with the country, with the habits of the animals and taught him to set traps and track foxes. He was not envious of Antony's success: on the contrary, he helped him prepare the pelts and was glad whenever he was more than ordinarily successful. Antony did not meet many people. Once out on the steppe, he saw two vagabonds, who, on perceiving him, began to ask for bread. He gave them his whole day's provisions and looked at them with sympathy. Perhaps a longing, like his own, drove them to choose this dreadful life.

Sometimes he met a fellow hunter, and they passed one another, each looking enviously at the other's bag of game. He learned that this man was a Tartar, and he kept a watchful eye on him, afraid, as most were, of a member of a generally feared nation. Most days, however, he did not see anyone. The loneliness and quiet of the country were like being in a great empty church. He walked there unseen, afraid to speak or to whistle. It seemed as though there he were in the very presence of the Almighty. The wind stopped his breath, the cold froze him to the bone, and the March sun was still without any warmth.

And thus, Antony hunted grey squirrels and learned

where to shoot ermine on the banks of the Tobol. Sometimes he killed a white fox, but he did not disdain the white rabbits, either, which swarmed on the steppe, and he set snares for partridges. He preserved the pelts and, every Sunday, went to the Kurhan market to dispose of his game. They did not pay much for it, but he was faithful to Shishkin's teaching and did not disdain any gain, however small.

In this way, he saved kopeks and roubles. Sometimes he counted his money and rejoiced at the thought of going back to his country. He drew up a plan that in the spring, as soon as there was grass, he would leave on his wagon, and he would drive it as far as possible and then sell it and the horse and continue his journey on foot, earning some money by working at anything he could find along the way to do. Perhaps by autumn, he would behold his country again. Once, when he had a great many skins, an opportunity came up to go to Tobolsk and sell them there. By then, he had fifty roubles and was very glad to count it.

He seldom indulged in any play, but one evening he went with some people to a dram shop and became quite talkative. He even laughed, and being animated by hope, he sang. He remembered his student days, his fiancee, his youth, and with a pure, strong voice, he sang in the empty street:

> *Lift up your glasses, comrades,*
> *And drink to the health of your sweethearts.*
> *Poor are those boys to whom the joy of love*
> *Is unknown.*

"The Lord be praised, but you are gay!" said someone behind him.

He stopped singing and saluted Marya. They walked on together, and he told her of his success.

"It is as though I had a hundred roubles, for the mare and the wagon are worth fifty. I will earn more before summer, and then I will go."

"That's nice. But you must keep out of bad company because it spoils your reputation. I had business with the tapster, and he said to me: 'What can be the matter with Mr. Mrozovetski that he keeps company with this bad lot?' These young people cause my father much sorrow; they are a disgrace to us. You must forgive me for speaking thus, but I should not like to have the same opinion of you that I have of your comrades."

"I thank you. I did not think of this, and indeed it was the first time I felt happy. I will promise you, just the same, never to see them again."

They parted at the door of the doctor's house, and the young man, still humming, returned home.

"There is a letter for you. I put it in your room," said Andryanek, half asleep, as he opened the door.

Antony's heart throbbed. He had had news a short time ago and did not expect to hear so soon again. He became frightened. He lit a candle. A white envelope, crumpled by its long journey and with several post-marks, lay on the table. His hands trembled as he impatiently opened it. It was from Valka and evidently written in a great hurry.

"DEAR ANTONY:

"We are in great trouble. For the past two weeks, Jozia has been very ill, and I can earn nothing as I am obliged to nurse her. Our lodgings are damp and poor, and the doctor has ordered her good air, quiet, and comfort. We are behind with our rent and cannot move as our savings are exhausted. Yesterday, to buy some food and medicine, I drew my last savings from the bank. This will last for a couple of weeks. I could have some money advanced by my employer, but I am afraid to ask, not knowing how soon I shall be able to return to my work. Poor Jozia knows nothing of my trouble, for I told her you had sent a hundred roubles. She is very weak and coughs constantly, but if she could only get what the doctor has prescribed, perhaps she might recover. She is so young and wishes so much to live! I am writing you all this so that you may not reproach me for having kept you in ignorance. I tried to get along as best I could without troubling you, but now I can do nothing more. The spring is very cold and damp. For Heaven's sake, let us hear from you; we are much worried on your account."

He laid his head on the table and, for a long time, sat motionless. It seemed to him that he was falling over a precipice and that something throbbed in his head and choked him. His frame was shaken with heavy sobs. The candle burned out, and still, he sat there in the darkness, fighting with his misery. Sorrow, the faithful companion of his life, again trampled him underfoot, laughing at his hopes and avenging itself for his brief moment of joy.

In the morning, he placed his fifty roubles in an envelope, wrote a bright, hopeful letter, and sent it by post. Then he took his rifle and escaped into the steppe. For three days, he shot nothing, and for three days, he ate nothing, nor did he speak a word.

Two weeks later, Miss Marya met him at the market in Kurhan, where he had brought his game to sell. He stood trembling in his worn-out sheep coat and felt boots and looked very miserable.

Towards evening, returning with goods for the store, she met him again. He was walking quickly on account of the cold.

She ordered the coachman to stop. "Sit here with me."

He sat with the coachman.

"You spare your horse too much," she said.

He shrugged his shoulders.

"I sold it," he answered abruptly.

"Why?"

"I needed the money."

"Have you invested it in some business? You did well! If you have good luck, you ought to double it before spring."

94

"I did not invest it," he whispered. "I sent it to the girls."

Then he became silent, staring over the steppe. She did not wish to question him further, and they arrived in Lebiazha in low spirits.

Another couple of weeks passed, and there arose a feeling in the air as though winter was tired at last, and the thermometer rose toward noon. The shanties standing on the Tobol were moved ashore; migrating fish appeared again in the river, and the skins of animals became worthless because their hair became thin and rough and shed in quantities. Tobolsk and even Kurhan swarmed with tradesmen eager to sell their wares to the Kirgiz. They spoke of caravans, pastures, and planting and looked toward the river and the south.

One Sunday, Antony went early to see the doctor. His eyes were red and burned feverishly. Quite a number of people were already present, so he asked Miss Marya to see him in another room.

"I should like to have the priest read a Requiem Mass for me today," he said sadly.

"Is it the anniversary of your parents' death?"

"No. My fiancee is dead."

"She has died?" Marya exclaimed.

He only nodded.

Then she understood his misery and the selling of the mare. Everything was gone.

"Poor fellow!" she said sympathetically. "I pity you with all my heart. Stay with us until after mass. Speak to us of your sorrow, and it will be easier to bear."

She pressed his hand and her eyes filled with tears.

Father Ubish read a Requiem Mass, and the lad prayed for the peace of the soul of the girl who had loved him, thus taking his farewell of her. She would have lived had his luck been better.

After dinner, when all the people had gone and the doctor had left to see Shishkin on some business, he told Miss

Marya everything. Little by little, a better and more cordial feeling had arisen between them, and it seemed to him only natural to tell her everything about himself. He spoke of his trouble quietly and with resignation.

"By the time I sent the fifty roubles I got for the mare, she had already died. My sister paid the funeral expenses with the money. She died of consumption. She was weak and exhausted from hard work. Valka is at work again. She cannot take a rest, as she has no more money, and I cannot send her more. She writes me that spring is already there, and she sent me some violets."

He took the letter from his pocket and handed Miss Marya the flowers, withered but still fragrant. Both smiled sadly.

"I shall never see fresh ones," he said. "I must stay here, it seems."

"What will you do?"

"I can earn my living with my gun. I don't need much. My sister is strong and healthy and can support herself. I must remain here," and he dropped his head on his breast.

He threw the flowers on the floor.

"I don't need the memory," he muttered.

CHAPTER VI
The Coming of Spring

AT last, the glorious spring days came, and the Siberian winter was gone. It did not retreat slowly as it does in the temperate climes, it did not offer a fight: it turned around and ran away, utterly crushed in the course of an afternoon.

Only the day before, a cold north wind blew, the snow lay heavy on the ground, and the ice was thick. But far to the south, in the warm desert, a mighty wind arose and rushed up north and fell like a hurricane upon the country. It came during the night and poured a stream of hot air over the ice and snow. And behold! In the morning, the Tobol shuddered and became dark. Then the ice broke, and from beneath it, water burst in jets. Floating chunks of ice commenced drifting northward, crushing, piling up on one another, crowding in on the shores, diving, and floating up, and announcing their march toward the north with a roar as of hundreds of cannons discharged all at once.

The mighty wind from the desert followed them, annihilating the snow on the steppe, striking the frozen swamp and the bunches of dried-up bushes, warming the hard ground, and hurrying on to the northern ocean.

Every year does the hot wind do this: attack the winter, create the spring, and then, in his turn, after five months, become the victim of the eternal ice of the far north. The following year his brother comes to avenge him and meet his doom in his turn. Thus this world was created so that even disinherited Siberia might have its summer. The Tobol now rushed toward the sea, dragging the ice with it, and the steppe poured into it its melted snows. The river became swollen, widened, and now looked like an ocean without shores. It lapped the feet of the levies and raced past villages throwing its foam over the houses. This lasted only a few days, after which the warm weather checked its speed, and then the river returned to its accustomed bounds to flow on lazily.

Within two days, the steppe turned black; in five, it showed first signs of life; in a week, it was green.

Mrozovetski, who beheld this miracle for the first time, thought of it as of a barbarian invasion. Like an invading horde, Nature knew no obstacle but rushed onward like a thunderbolt, crushing everything in her path, then falling asleep when the impetuous rush was over. As man springs from Nature, so he is like the soil on which he lives.

The warm weather came on at once. The steppe, saturated with moisture, began to tremble and live. Everything grew with wonderful rapidity. It seemed as though the noise of the growing shrubs and the bursting buds could be heard, and the growth of the leaves seen. Immediately the formerly empty places were filled with people. The Kirgiz folded up their yurts and, leaving their winter quarters, rushed away to the south, taking with them their sheep, cattle, and horses.

They were followed, as armies are by vultures, by caravans of merchants selling cotton goods. They marched on in large tribes, fully armed, and took with them people—all hands not tied down to agricultural work. At their head was a trustworthy guide familiar with the steppe and the customs of its wild inhabitants.

In a couple of weeks, there remained in Kvasnikoffs' house only the patriarch of the family and Antony, the sons all having scattered over the steppe with their wives. The old man watched the house and office, and Antony, having no other occupation, worked by day in the gardens and fields. Hunting has stopped. He had no money to buy the necessary articles for fishing and was obliged to earn his living as best he could. In the beginning, the work was hard, but necessity forced him to it. He worked with an aching neck and feeble arms.

Mrs. Utovich called him to work in her garden because while he worked, she could talk. Gossiping was her first and greatest weakness; her second was avarice. She boarded her workman but said nothing about paying him. The doctor and his daughter had gone to Tobolsk, so the old woman had everything her own way and introduced new economies. Antony was ashamed to ask for his pay. This lasted until the doctor returned.

Miss Marya was surprised to see that, notwithstanding the heat, he worked in his old *tulub*. He did not even remove it during dinner, though they served him in the very warm kitchen.

"Come upstairs," she called to him.

"No, thank you, I am very dirty,'" he said, blushing.

He went back to his work. Toward evening handed Mrs. Utovich thirty kopeks for him, but the old woman said:

"It's not necessary. He is working for his board. He did not ask for pay. Besides, he doesn't work well; he has no gardening experience."

"How many days have you had him work here?"

"Five."

The girl shrugged her shoulders. When he had finished his work, she called him to the store and counted out ten zloty.[24]

"That's for your work in the garden," she said. "And for your driving last winter, there are four roubles coming to you. Here they are." "Less thirty kopeks," he said, pushing back the

---

[24] 1 zloty was equal 15 kopeks

silver coin. The rest he took and said:

"I know that I am a very poor gardener. I really don't know the first thing about it. Perhaps you don't care to have me come anymore?"

"What an idea! It is hard for a student of technology to become a gardener all at once, but you will learn in time."

"That's true. Then I shall go mowing. I can't do any other work during the summer. Hunting doesn't pay in the summer. Nobody buys the birds, and the skins are no good."

He leaned on the counter and still lingered.

"I had a letter from my sister," he said.

"How is she?" Marya asked.

"Not very well. She has some debts."

He pulled a letter from his pocket.

"You haven't seen any lilac for a long time," he said with a smile. "Here is some she sent."

With hands trembling from hard work, he gave her a dried stem.

"How lovely," she said, caressing the withered flowers.

He blushed.

"Sister begged me to give it to you from her, with her thanks for the trouble you took while I was sick. It's a little nothing, but we had nothing better to offer."

"It is more welcome than anything else."

She placed the flowers between the pages of a book and said:

"You had better bring your sister here. Together, you will be able to get along better; and then you don't need a million rubles to go back."

He laughed softly as though it were a good joke.

"Certainly. Instead of trying to recover Promieniev through court proceedings, it would be easier to purchase it from Burski and become a landlord that way."

"Don't laugh. In ten years, you may become a millionaire. Smolin was a penniless clerk ten years ago, and look at him now. One sees such miracles often here; only one must have perseverance."

He did not laugh anymore but looked at her, wondering whether she mocked him.

Then he sighed, put the letter and the money in his pocket, and prepared to go. In doing so, his overcoat opened, and she saw that his clothing and linen were in rags. Now she understood why he never took off his tulub.

Two days later, she found a piece of paper on the kitchen table, which, on examination, she discovered to be the post-office receipt for four roubles sent to Valerya Mrozovetski. She put this in the book with the lilac, saying to herself:

"Oh, anima vilis."

Since the arrival of spring, few people gathered in the doctor's house on Sundays. Those who had money had rented a piece of land, and being agricultural people for generations, they farmed it with great enthusiasm. The young men had been engaged by the merchants to go into the steppe with the caravans to trade. Only the old and the sick remained, or the lazy ones, or those restless souls who could not warm a place anywhere for very long. A few men of this sort stopped Antony on the banks of the Tobol and tried to induce him to go to a dram shop. They were already drunk, and when he resisted, they began to push him into the river, half in joke, half in earnest. He resisted as long as he could, but finally, he stumbled over a stone, and, holding onto two of his aggressors, he tumbled into the river. Some fisherman, attracted by the commotion, arrived on the scene and pulled them out, barely alive. Their bath sobered up his tormentors, and they apologized, afraid that he might press charges, but they did not offer to pay him for his *tulub*, which was ruined by the water. He dried it and almost wept when he found he could make no further use of it, for he had nothing else to wear.

Old Kvasnikoff looked at him out of the corner of his eye.

"You are a stupid boy," he said at last. "It would be a bad summer indeed if you could not earn enough money for another *tulub*. Throw it away, and if you haven't the money to buy some cotton for a shirt, take mine."

In this way, for the first time, Antony was dressed like a Siberian peasant. For some time, he could not get used to the pink shirt, but he grew accustomed to it eventually, as he had grown used to many other things. Now the work was easier, his arms and neck became tougher and more muscular, and he himself grew stronger. He gave up all his brilliant projects and became too stupefied to even feel sorrow keenly. He thought only of one thing: how to earn his bread for the next day. He worked like an animal.

One evening he called at Gostinskis'. He went there mechanically, thinking that perhaps they would give him some work. Passing the kitchen, he greeted Father Ubish, who seemed not to recognize him, passed Mrs. Utovich, who was busy in the store, and went upstairs.

The doctor was in his office and said to him at once,

"Antony, will you do me a favor?"

"Anything you ask."

"Will you go into the steppe with *litovki*?"

"What do you mean by *litovki*?"

"Scythes. I bought three wagons of them. Now someone must go out into the steppe with them and travel from village to village, from farm to farm, to sell them."

The boy hesitated.

"It means the handling of quite a lot of money, and I might be robbed along the way."

"You will have ten men with you."

"But I am not familiar with the villages and roads."

"I'll send Grinya with you. He's done the route with me four years in a row. He will show you the way, and your escort will defend you in case you are attacked. You will be away all summer and return home at the close of the fall. I would go myself, but I am getting too old."

"I will as you say, but..."

"Wait, I know all about the 'buts.' You will get five kopeks commission on every scythe you sell, plus your traveling expenses. You will have to take care of everything: feed the people, take command, and see that they do not steal. Tonight you will see your people, select your horses and pack for the trip. You must start the day after tomorrow, for, at any moment now, the grass will be ready to mow."

"I am ready and willing to serve you, but I am afraid I may not be equal to the task."

"That is silly talk, my dear boy. You know addition and subtraction, and you know how to make change for a rouble. You cannot work in the garden forever. Well, then, don't talk nonsense, but sit down and have supper with me. In a few moments, all your men will be here. You know them all but one."

In fact, they were all old acquaintances: Rudnicki, Czyż, Stasiak, and some neighboring peasants. They sat down at the table without ceremony and filled the whole house with their free, loud talk.

At length, a stranger appeared. He was a tall, blonde young fellow.

"Good evening!" he said.

The doctor brought him to Antony.

"Here is your last companion. He is a countryman of yours. His name is Andukaytis."

They shook hands, looking into each other's eyes. The newcomer then sat down at the table and ate enough for three men without saying a word. Mrozovetski liked him instantly, for he also preferred to remain silent. They drank lots of tea and then went out to rest. Only Antony remained for further instructions, and none of them slept much that night, the women being busy preparing provisions and other articles necessary for the journey into the steppe. The doctor urged them on, giving instructions, Mrs. Utovich scolded, Antony placed the packages in the hall, and the drunken Sergey sang to Katalay. Miss Marya spoke little but worked the hardest.

"This is for you," she said, handing Antony a large package. "You must take this *tulub* because, in the fall, the nights are cold. Don't refuse, please. You will find it in your bill, and we will settle up later, but you can't go without clothing."

"Perhaps when I return, you will not be here anymore."

"Oh, I am my father's immovable real estate. Only death can take me away from here."

"May the Lord preserve you!" he exclaimed.

She shrugged her shoulders.

"Nobody would be sorry. It makes no difference to anyone whether I die or not."

Her eyes flashed angrily, so he said nothing.

The following day, when the doctor went to wake him, he found him already in the courtyard. With Grinya's aid, they pulled out all the wagons and prepared for the journey. First, there were barrels with scythes; then, they began to load other bundles of goods to sell: dishes and tools. At about noon, all the men showed up. Then Shumski appeared unexpectedly to lunch. He criticized everything and jokingly incited the men against Antony. The peasants did not pay any attention to this, but the Poles at once began to trifle with their superior, who patiently endured everything. Only Andukaytis took his side. With his mouth full of bread, he turned toward Shumski and said:

"If you know everything better, why don't you go instead of us? The doctor knew whom he wished to trust. With God's help, we won't get lost."

Again he and Antony looked into each other's eyes and felt they were friends.

After lunch, the doctor said:

"Well, you must be going. You will pass the night on the steppe."

"Let us see this procession," said Shumski, lighting a cigarette.

He went out into the yard, humming gaily.

He was dressed elegantly and looked very sharp.

Antony took command. Grinya drove the first troika, and with him sat Czyż and two Siberian peasants. They pulled out onto the road.

The peasant Porfiry drove the second troika, and three men were with him. The third troika was driven by Rudnicki. Andukaytis drove the fourth.

Antony wiped his forehead, shook his hands with the doctor and the others, saluted Shumski from afar, then, gathering up the reins, he moved on.

"Holy Joseph, protect them!" shouted Mrs. Utovich.

"Antony, take care!" shouted the doctor.

"Have you taken your rifle?" asked Marya.

"Thank you, yes," he answered, taking off his cap to greet her.

They drove down the street, watched by the whole household. Even Father Ubish appeared much interested in the expedition. He rubbed his hands and laughed. Antony turned several times, then whipped up the horses to overtake the others, and dust covered everything. The doctor returned to the house with Shumski, talking about the business on the steppe, and only the priest and Miss Marya remained in the street. He turned toward the girl and whispered:

"They went away. They did well. Don't say a word, but it is true."

Then he blushed and kicked the ground with his foot.

"I have had enough of it myself. If you like to stay here, very well, but I shall not stay. I have had enough of it. Remain in good health. I am going to my parish."

He commenced to gesticulate and went straight down the road, talking to himself. "They have nothing here! No organ, only two chasubles, and never a procession. I have had enough of such penance. I was not consecrated a priest for such shabby business! I shall find my way. I will show them that I can find it!"

"Dinner is ready!" said Miss Marya.

This usually quieted the demented man, but today it had no effect on him, and Miss Marya stepped back into the house.

"Father! Father Ubish has had an attack and has gone off. You had better call him."

"Oh, this is not the first time. He will come back when he gets hungry," said the doctor, and Marya shrugged her shoulders.

"As you say," she muttered.

And the poor old priest trotted on further and further, led on by one thought. And he soon disappeared on the steppe.

CHAPTER VII
A Summer on the Steppe

THE grass was ready for mowing and the whole steppe, from Tobolsk to Tashkent, was one beautiful sea of greens and flowers. It stood in the blazing sun, completely motionless, unstirred by even the faintest breeze. Here and there stood an island of birches, hawthorn, or the snow-white meadowsweet on which the eye, tired by the monotony of the green verdure, rested with relief.

The villages were scattered all over the steppe and far apart from one another, often separated by dozens and scores of versts of utter wilderness. And in-between, people, laws, and boundaries were forgotten, and one was reminded of the pre-historic times of which the Bible speaks—of million-headed herds, ancient patriarchs, and a virgin country that had never seen a man. Here, without count or measure, the soil yielded an abundance of grass, in which lurked innumerable birds and beasts. And over everything stood the burning sun, the cloudless sky, and not a breath of air was stirring.

What people were obliged to work hard for in other lands was given here freely, sowed by the munificent hand of Nature, which, like the hand of a rich man, cares not where it throws its riches. There was an abundance of flax, wild asparagus, beans, wild strawberries, and cherries which belonged to nobody but the birds of the sky or the man who would extend his hand for them. In some places, the earth, burned by the sun, and bulging from the excess of power, split into deep crevices, whilst in others, the grass shone with drops of dew, glistening like jewels. In some places, the steppe, as though hiding from the sun, ran into deep ravines, where it was quickly entangled in the thickets of hawthorn and meadowsweet. These ravines were noisy with the cries of the white partridge and red-breasted *galanduks*.

The government road, marked with posts, ran over the steppe, branching out constantly into thousands of smaller tracks. It extended over hundreds and thousands of versts and, like a great artery, and carried the strength, the life, and thought of the steppes far, far away to China.

The steppe cared not for borders or human roads but extended toward the Tobol, its other powerful artery, also carrying the strength and thought of Nature: water. The steppe was thirsty and therefore reached out toward the river, which fortified itself against the onslaught of the thirsty aggressor behind a chain of alluvial hills, thickly clad with pine trees, as though it were afraid of being devoured by the grass and thickets of the steppe.

The whole steppe was broken by these hills. Nature denied it brooks and springs and gave it only lakes of both fresh and salt water. Those of salt water were deserted, despised even by grass, but about the freshwater lakes, birds swarmed, trees sprung up, and foliage flourished, making these appear like temples of a beneficent Deity, where the steppe came to worship.

When Antony and his escort turned from the government road onto the small tracks connecting various villages and farms, his soul became strangely gay. He felt stronger and as free as a bird. He was suddenly filled with energy and joy. The love of life and action returned to him. And he had plenty of hard work to expend that energy. They stopped at villages to transact business. The peasants surrounded the wagon, testing the scythes and bargaining: their arrival became a regular market day.

They had to keep a sharp look-out for counterfeit banknotes, which circulated throughout the country in large quantities, and it was often necessary to take their pay in the products of Nature—salt, skins, and grains of gold, and sometimes to give credit, writing down the name of the purchaser so as to be able to find him on their return in the fall.

Having learned the value of his men, Antony had divided among them what work there was to do. Czyż, a man of great experience, who, during his twenty years of life in Siberia, had manufactured salt, dug gold, sold skins, and traded with the Kirgiz, helped him in conducting transactions. Rudnicki was made the overseer of the horses, wagons, and provisions. Stasiak prepared the camp, and Andukaytis was their cook and purchaser of foodstuffs. The peasants loaded and unloaded, pitched camps, collected firewood, and saw to the horses, and they constituted their defense against tramps and Tartars.

After a couple of weeks, everything went smoothly, each one attending to his duties. Antony's careful attention to business and his kindness in dealing with his men won over even the most rebellious among them. He seldom commanded, he found a simple request was usually enough, and so harmony reigned among these widely different people gathered together from all nations. They went further and further into the steppe, toward the east and south, occasionally meeting the Cossack mounted police, who defended the land from Kirgiz marauders. They reached farms where the people dwelt as though on remote islands; they visited villages whose inhabitants went to the city once a year on the day of the fair.

Usually, they camped wherever the night overtook them. At such times, they circled the wagons close together, hobbled the horses and let them out to pasture, and searched for water. If they found no lake, they used the water they carried with them in barrels. They cooked their meals over a fire built of dried scrub, which they collected in the steppe, and boiled the water for their tea in the samovar, lighting their pipes after the meal.

Then everyone, having fulfilled his duty, rested or occupied himself according to his taste. Some ate and drank, others crawled into the wagons and went to sleep, and others talked and laughed. Czyż amused them by relating stories he had gathered from all parts of Siberia; Grinya played on the balalaika simple, monotonous Siberian melodies. Andukaytis ate in silence or, though this was very seldom, sang sacred songs after he had finished his meal. Antony checked the camp and his people and, by moonlight, made up his accounts. He placed the banknotes in a leather bag that he carried on his breast, and he kept the coins in a large calfskin bag. Then he relaxed in his own way: he took his rifle and went out on the steppe. He was very fond of the beauties of Nature, of the tranquility and majesty of this great desert, and he loved the never-ending green sea of grass. Every day he discovered new charms, new surprises, and new riches.

When supper was ready, Andukaytis called him by whistling, which was taken up by the echo and repeated to infinity, and only then he returned to camp. He was courteous but distant to his comrades. Only Andukaytis was at all familiar with him. So many months spent in one wagon! Under these circumstances, the most diffident would become familiar. At noon, as they drove slowly along, the men drowsy with the heat, Andukaytis would light his pipe and chat, and soon Antony learned why he had been sent to Siberia. His sentence was for six years. He related the story with much gusto, laughing all the while.

"It was on account of Kmita. He was a great horse thief. He stole hundreds of horses. When he was caught, he was sentenced to a long time in prison, but when his term was over, he came out and began to steal again. This was too much for us, and we organized a court in the village and passed the death sentence on him.

"This was all very well: we all wanted to kill him, but no one wished to do it himself. Finally, we agreed to draw lots. We threw some wheat straws into a cap and, among them, one buckwheat straw. And wouldn't you know it, I drew the buckwheat. So, I set out, taking a horse bridle with me, and went after him. At length, I came across him on the bank of our holy river.[25] I sprang at his throat, and he put a knife into my side. I threw him to the ground, and he stabbed me in the leg."

Here he opened his mouth and showed his teeth like a wolf, laughing softly.

"I finally got the bridle round his neck, and he bit my arm like a wild horse. No matter, I bound it up, tied the reins around his neck, and drowned him in the river."

Here he knocked the ashes from his pipe and, being always hungry, began to eat a piece of bread with relish.

"They found his body in the river and tried to discover the murderer. Nobody suspected me. I lay in bed, waiting for my wounds to heal. But I had taken his knife as a keepsake, and my youngest brother found it and took it out with him when he played in the street. Someone recognized it, and—I was taken. When I got well, they sent me here. No matter, only I am lonesome for my mama."

He often spoke about "mama," and the others teased him continually, calling him "little orphan boy." He was very useful in the caravan. He cooked and purchased their provisions; he even did the washing. He was as peaceful as a lamb and got along with everyone. To look at him, no one would believe that he was a murderer. But he bore the marks of his fight and was lame in one foot from Kmita's knife. He had also lost one finger, which the thief had bitten off.

---

[25] The River Neman, the main river artery of the former Duchy of Lithuania

He did not dislike his life in Siberia. Seeing the different people amused him, and the stoic philosophy of the peasants helped him in his moments of misery. To be happy, he needed only a large quantity of bread. When he was not hungry, he did the work of three men, and when he was hungry, he slept.

One night, in their wanderings, they passed one night in a ravine where a solitary *futor*[26] stood. The farmer had chosen a good position. In front of his house was a small lake of fresh water and, not far distant—a grove of birch trees. The house was surrounded by a deep ditch, around which was a raised levy surmounted by a strong fence of hawthorn wood.

Antony's men pitched their camp not far from the lake, and men and their horses quenched their thirst, then they built a fire. No one appeared from the farmhouse, so they, for their part, did not make any haste to pay their neighbor a visit.

After supper, Antony went out on the steppe as usual. The evening was lovely, and the cool breeze refreshing after the hot day. At the least noise, *tarbagans*[27] sprang from the grass and ran away. In the bushes, the partridges called their mates to sleep.

Antony, humming, went toward the grove of birch trees. Suddenly he saw something white among the trees and stood still. Someone rose from the ground. Antony raised his rifle but soon lowered it, seeing that it was a woman picking berries. The earth was red with them, and her overturned basket testified to her fright. Antony spoke to her in a friendly way, and he also began to pick berries. The woman, reassured, approached him, and they looked at each other, first diffidently, out of the corners of their eyes, then more boldly.

The blood mounted to the boy's cheeks, for the girl was gorgeous. She was slender and beautifully proportioned; she seemed like a goddess of the virginal steppe. Her hair was deep

---

[26] A fortified farmhouse in the steppe
[27] Tarbagan marmot—a large steppe rodent

gold, and her eyes grey-blue, like flax flowers. Her complexion was sun-kissed and warm with the blood of youth. Her sunburned hands and bare feet were small and exquisitely formed. She did not look frightened and gazed upon him in curiosity, for where she lived, she seldom saw strangers. She recommenced picking berries and was the first to speak.

" Are you come to the shaman on business?"'

"Then this is the shaman's *futor*?"

"Yes. He is at home."

"Are you his daughter?"

"No. He bought me at the fair."

"Where?"

"At Tobolsk. It was five years ago. My brother sold me to him for eight years."

"Why?"

"To be his servant. He gave thirty roubles for me. My brother told him he would buy me back when he had the money. He was a gold smuggler; perhaps he was successful, and his comrades killed him. I have not heard from him since."

"What was your brother's name?"

"Franek Shishko. I am Zosha Shishko."

"Then you are not a Siberian?"

"No. I am from Poland. But I was very small when my brother brought me here. Now I am eighteen."

"Do you like living here?"

"Very much. They respect me because I do my work well, and they know I will not steal from them."

"The shaman has a wife?"

"No. A housekeeper."

She shrugged her shoulders contemptuously, gathered up her basket, and turned to go.

"Are you a hunter?" she asked. "No. I am selling *litovki*."

"I am glad to hear it. I must buy one. It is time for mowing."

"Do you mow, too?"

"There is no one else to do it. The shaman is constantly away on the road, and the old woman looks after the cows. I plow and mow, and the old people make butter and cheese."

She spoke of doing the plowing and mowing as though it were a very natural thing for a girl. Tall and strong, she looked like a good worker. Her young chest rose and fell slowly, and her form indicated strength and flexibility acquired by continual outdoor exercise. Her well-poised head had an air of untamed freedom and energy. She looked at him again.

"What is your name?"

He told her, and she was thoughtful for a while.

"Then you are not a Siberian, either?" '

"No. I am your brother, you might say."

She laughed, showing her splendid white teeth.

"Let us then converse in our own tongue. I have almost forgotten it. Come to the *futor,* and I will give you something to eat."

"I am not alone. Ten of my men are camping near the lake."

At that moment, he heard Andukaytis's whistle.

"They are calling me."

"I will see you again then. I must buy a *litovka.*"

"Let us go together. I must see the shaman, for we must be on the move tomorrow morning!"

He preferred looking at the girl to doing any business.

As they approached the farm, she stopped.

"Don't speak in our language in the presence of the shaman. He doesn't like it."

They entered the yard, where several cows stood just brought from the pasture. Two people were milking them: they were the shaman and an old Siberian woman.

"Master," called the girl. "Merchants selling scythes are camping near the lake."

"Why did you let them in?" came a voice which Antony recognized. "They will cut our grass or steal something."

114

"Pshaw!" laughed the girl. "Don't be afraid. Better buy me a scythe."

"And where is the old one?"

"You may mow with the old one. I can't. The merchant is here. Come and see him."

From behind the cows, the shaman, lame and bent, hobbled toward Antony.

"How do you do, Antony Stefanovich?" he said.

"Ah, you recognize me. And how do you know my father's name?"

"Someone told me. Come in, please. I have nothing. I am a poor man, but still, I invite you to my miserable dwelling. Well, you are already selling scythes: you are fortunate."

"The scythes are not mine. Will you buy a couple?"

"I haven't a kopek."

"Then give me a rouble if you have no kopeks."

"One rouble for a scythe! Great Lord! I pay much less in Tobolsk."

"Well, I brought the scythe to your house. But there, do as you please. If you wish to go to Tobolsk to fetch your own at a lower price, I will not insist."

They entered the house, which was plastered outside with loam, and hung inside with felt. It looked like a big molehill, but there was plenty of room and light inside. In the windows, in place of glass, there were sheets of mica, and the furniture was solid and comfortable. Antony seated himself on a bench, his rifle in his hand. This shaman, notwithstanding his feeble appearance, frightened him and filled him with diffidence. Looking at him, he could not rid himself of the impression that the man was an enormous spider looking for his prey.

"Maybe we can bargain over the scythe?" the shaman said, looking sidewise at the young man.

"How?"

"I will furnish you with milk. You have ten people, and

they must drink a lot. Whose merchandise is it?"

"The doctor's, from Lebiazha."

It seemed to him that the shaman's face turned sallow.

"He does good business and is much respected by his people. He's lucky! Most men die beggars, but he will leave a fortune!"

"Do you know him?"

"Oh, I know him. He dragged me into court on account of some herbs I sold to the peasants. I was in prison for two months, and then they flogged me. But they don't dare to strike him, although he is an exile like me. He is lucky!"

He said this calmly, but his hooked fingers picked nervously at his *khalat*. Antony shuddered, thinking how threatening the man appeared. At that moment, the girl entered the room, and instinctively he felt that no harm could come to him in her presence.

"I shut the door, but there is a man knocking at it. It must be one of yours," she said, turning toward Mrozovetski. "I told him he needn't worry about you, but he doesn't believe me."

"Don't let him in," said the old man.

"I will go to him myself," said Antony rising.

"Have you bought me a scythe? I am going to fetch it," said the girl.

"I didn't buy one. They are too dear. We can get along without it."

"Indeed? I told you to give the merchant a sable skin for it if you have no cash. But I know you have it: why hang onto your money like that? You can't eat it."

"Oh, be silent! I am a beggar. Who told you I had any money!"

"Eh!" muttered the girl. "I don't talk when I know I ought not to, but this merchant is a countryman of mine, and he will not do us any harm. Well, give him a sable skin, and I will go and pick out a scythe. They are going away early tomorrow

116

morning."

She spoke quickly and with determination, but the shaman did not budge.

"Will you trust me?" he said to Antony. "I will pay you in the autumn. You will be coming back this way on your way to Lebiazha."

"Very well, but you will then have to pay one rouble and a half. Such are my orders because we lose a great deal on credit sales."

"He will pay," said the girl softly, "and if he does not, I will pay. Let us be going."

The old man remained silent as a protest against these proceedings.

Antony went out with the girl and said to her softly:

"It seems to me that I shall have to make you a present of the scythe. Well, so let it be. I will pay the doctor, and you shall thank me."

She looked at him with her clear eyes but said nothing.

Andukaytis was rapping continuously at the door. On seeing the girl, he ceased.

"*Grazhi mergayte!*"[28] he muttered in Lithuanian.

They went to the camp. Everyone was asleep except Czyż, who kept the watch alone.

"Be careful in your dealings with the shaman," he said, "or he will steal your shirt. He is worse than a Kirgiz."

Antony did not answer. He led the girl to the wagon, where the scythes were, and picked out the best for her. Then they both turned in the direction of the farm. The night was almost as clear as day, and the steppe was quiet. They lowered their voices and spoke in their own tongue. She spoke of her work and he of his long journey. Then she asked him about his people and listened as though he told her some news. When they reached the door, they stopped.

---

[28] How do you do?

"I don't remember anything about our country. A strange, different country. Tell me, how is it?" she asked.

"There is not such a heavy winter, and there are many more people. The trees and flowers are different. In the villages, there are churches, and all fields are cultivated. In the cities, the streets are paved, and the houses are of stone."

"And they all speak our language?"

"All."

She gazed into space and whispered, "I would like to see it!"

Then she asked suddenly:

"Do they sing there? Sing something for me, will you?"

He began to hum:

I sowed the wheat in the field,
But cannot reap it at all.
I was in love with a girl,
But her I could not win.

Because one sows
but may not reap.
Because one loves
but may not win.

Though she rejected me,
I will not ever curse her!"

"Lock the door, and let loose the dogs!" called the shaman from the inside.

The girl made an involuntary movement as though she had been listening to unknown sounds. He took her hand:

"Goodbye," he whispered. "Don't forget me. I shall never forget you. I will be back in the fall."

She turned toward him and looked steadily into his eyes with a sorrowful gaze.

"It's too bad," she whispered.

"May the scythe serve you well, and while mowing... remember my song."

Then he clasped her in his arms and kissed her.

The girl trembled and grew pale.

Once a hunter who passed the night on the farm had tried to kiss her. At that time, she had been so angry and revolted that she wished to strangle the man with her strong hands. But the man who kissed her now was a countryman. She did not strike him, nor did she call him a beast. She only pushed his face gently away from hers and retreated quietly to the door.

"Goodbye, Zosha," he whispered. "Remember me and keep well."

She locked the door and let loose the dogs, but she did not go into the house. She leaned on the gate and looked toward the camp, where the fire, replenished from time to time, was burning brightly. She heard Grinya's balalaika, and when he stopped playing, she heard the second verse of Antony's song:

The wheat grew up
but before the harvest
It was laid low by hail,
My love laid low by gossip.

My wheat laid low by hail,
I did not win the girl.
Though she rejected me,
I think of her with joy.

The following day no trace of the wanderers remained, save only for trampled grass and cold ashes. They had disappeared into the steppe.

It was a very brief episode in Antony's life, but it was pregnant in consequences, and could he have foreseen them, he would probably have avoided the shaman's *futor*. But it was his destiny to pass through all the torments of hell.

Everything went satisfactorily on his journey. Business was excellent, and the grass had already begun to brown by the time he sold his last scythe. He sent home two empty wagons and seven of the men. Grinya, Andukaytis, and Rudnicki remained with him, and in their company, he began his return trip, collecting the money for the scythes sold on credit. They took a zig-zag route, stopping here and there. There was little trouble with the collections—the Siberians are generally honest and reliable. They paid promptly and received Antony and his companions hospitably. Although it was only the end of July, the nights were already cold, and in places, the foliage was already falling. On this account, they did not pass the nights on the steppe, which had its riches and life but which offered no shelter—they slept with the farmers in their huts or in the stables.

The more delicate plants had already withered from the cold of the night, but the hardier ones stood brown and bare, scattering their seeds and shedding their leaves. Of the snow-white meadowsweet, nothing remained but dry brambles. The birds were silent, the *tarbagans* hid in their holes. It was as though sadness and fear seized the heart of nature before the approaching winter.

But Antony's heart was joyful. He was gay and happy. He laughed at the slightest provocation, whistled, sang, and played about like a boy. The expedition had been successful, and his leather bag was full of money. The horses and men were in good health, and his soul was filled with great joy.

When he thought of the young girl at the *futor*, his heart throbbed, and his blood grew warmer, and something seemed to draw him to her, whispering to him during his sleeping hours and accompanying him during the day. As they drew nearer the *futor*, he could hardly restrain his impatience: he wished to fly there.

Finally, the last intervening night passed. Jack Frost

covered the earth, and their breath froze in the air. Yet, Antony felt warm. One hundred versts separated them from the *futor*. They covered them by sunset, and Antony saw the shaman's farm from far off and hurried their horses. They stopped before the locked gate, and the boy jumped down from horseback. He wished to call, but they had already been seen. The gate opened, and Zosha appeared. She was dressed in a *tulub* and long felt boots. About her head was tied a red kerchief. They gazed at each other and smiled joyfully.

"Come right in. The shaman is not at home."

This was the acme of good luck. The men drew the wagon into the yard, and Antony and the girl entered the large room. The old witch peered at them with her gloomy eyes, half hidden beneath bushy eyebrows, and then quickly left the room.

Presently Andukaytis entered and, greeting the girl after his rough fashion, said,

"I want some bread!"

"I should prefer some tea with vodka," said Rudnicki, who came in behind him.

"It is very cold," announced Grinya, entering last.

He looked about the room and spat on the floor.

"A devil, not a man! There is not one holy icon in the house."

This put him out of humor for the whole evening.

The young girl set the vodka on the table, prepared tea, and brought bread, cedar nuts, and cold roast lamb, which she placed on the table.

"What a pretty girl," said Rudnicki.

"If she had dark eyes and hair, I would fall in love with her," added Andukaytis, chewing his bread.

She laughed but said nothing. After a while, the old witch returned. She glanced at the abundantly spread table and trembled with indignation, but she said nothing, only whispered to the girl:

"I will serve the tea."

Antony sat not far from the table, gazing at the girl. She seated herself beside him, and they began to talk quietly. Rudnicki elbowed Andukaytis.

"They are friends already," he whispered.

The Samogitian[29] laughed softly and said:

"Let them be if they like it. I prefer the bread."

They ate everything on the table, then Andukaytis asked Antony:

"Is there any work to do?"

"No," he answered, distracted.

"Then I am going to sleep because I have had enough to eat."

"We also," said Rudnicki and Grinya and discreetly took their leave.

The old woman lit an oil lamp and beckoned to them to pass to the other side of the hall. The large room was lost in darkness. The young people drew closer to each other and whispered softly and then more softly still. Then the old woman came back, placed the lamp on the table, poured out a glass of tea, and invited Antony to drink.

"Oh, my, my! You must be hungry!" exclaimed the girl.

"Not very. I can eat tomorrow, and God only knows when I shall see you again."

He rose, just the same, and drank the tea down in a few gulps.

"You will come again? It's only three hundred versts from here to Lebiazha."

"Certainly I will. I will buy a horse at once and come here every other week."

"I will ask the old man to allow me to go to Lebiazha to mass from time to time. I have lived like a godless beast here, but from today it will be different."

---

[29] Samogitia is one of the five historical regions of Lithuania proper

"Of course, it will be different. In a year or so, as soon as I set aside enough money, I will marry you."

"We needn't much. Have we not strong arms? And will you take me back to our country?"

"I will take you there, but it cannot be soon."

"We can wait," she answered courageously.

They chatted thus for some time, and Antony drank another glass of tea. He felt strangely tired and grew very sleepy. His eyelids closed, and his head drooped. The girl noticed this, and placed several sheepskins on the bench for him, brought him a pillow, bade him good night, and left him alone, taking the lamp with her. She did not notice the dark shadow lurking behind the stove and watching them. And neither did Antony. He was so sleepy that, without undressing, he threw himself on the improvised bed and slept like a log.

The next morning, Andukaytis could hardly wake him. The wagon was ready, and the Samogitian urged him to depart at once. Antony felt as though he had been tipsy. His head ached, and his legs felt like lead. The young girl gave him some tea and advised him to rest, but he was again seized with fear of this house and its inhabitants. Zosha accompanied him quite a distance from the *futor* and then returned alone, having again received his promise to come to see her in a couple of weeks. Not until evening did Antony begin to feel better.

"You must be coming down with fever," his comrades decided. It was their last night on the road, so they were in good spirits. Each one of them expected to find some news from home awaiting him in Lebiazha. They counted their gains and spoke of taking a long rest after the hard work of the summer. Antony estimated that he had earned about one hundred roubles. He would buy a horse, and during the winter, he would earn his living by driving and thus be able to see the girl very often. They urged on the horses, and their wagon sped over the frozen ground. Gradually, they began to see people out on the steppe, and it was dusk when, with a great noise and loud singing, they entered Lebiazha. Their acquaintances greeted them heartily. Tomoy recognized Antony and, squealing continually, accompanied him home.

Without knowing why the boy shuddered as he opened the gate of the doctor's house. Was it joy, or uneasiness, or a presentiment?

Mrs. Utovich rushed out first, and behind her came the doctor.

"Antony, you all return well?"

"Thank God, we do!" said Mrozovetski.

"Come in. Come in. Everything went well?"

"All well," he answered. "One minute. I will put the horses in the stable and bring the haul."

Soon, he went into the house. Ragged and dirty, with long unkempt hair, he looked like a tramp, as Shumski immediately remarked.

He entered the room, carrying the bags of copper, and threw them on the floor of the doctor's room. Then he removed the bag with paper money from his neck and placed it on the desk.

His eyes laughed with honest joy when he looked on the familiar faces and furniture, and even Shumski appeared agreeable to him at that moment.

"And where is our priest?" he asked.

"He went away and... never came back," answered the doctor gloomily.

"Poor man, he went in search of his parish."

"One madman less," said Shumski. "I am sure they murdered him for his boots. He caused us much trouble, though, for we shall now be obliged to wait with the wedding until we can find another priest."

"Then there is no more mass on Sunday?"

"We read the prayers ourselves," said Miss Marya. "We cannot, however, have the sacrament administered to us."

"What a pity," muttered Antony.

"What need have you for sacraments?" laughed Shumski. "So, tell us, have you found a sweetheart on the steppe?"

The boy blushed and fell silent.

Happily, Rudnicki, the great gossip, was gone, and Andukaytis was eating and made no haste to tell of the shaman's *futor*. Only Miss Marya noticed the blush and his embarrassment, but she said nothing. After supper, they went into the doctor's office. Antony wished to retire.

"If you will allow me," he said, "I should like to reckon up with you tonight. I shall sleep better. Then I will go home as I expect to find a letter from my sister there."

"Very well. Let us count up."

They poured out the coins, and all began to count. He had received three thousand roubles' worth of merchandise and now presented his accounts.

"Very economically managed," said the doctor looking over the accounts with clear pleasure.

Then they counted the salary of the escort, half of which had already been paid by Antony, and the value of the raw products received in exchange.

"Very good! I see you will yet be a businessman yet! They have not cheated you," said the doctor joyfully, weighing the grains of gold while Miss Marya and Shumski examined the skins.

"I have fifteen hundred roubles in my bag," said Antony proudly, taking out the bundles of banknotes.

The doctor took the first package and began to count it. Suddenly he stopped, shook his head, looked at a banknote carefully, took it to light, and then dropped his hands.

Antony looked at him.

"Where did you change this money?" asked the doctor.

"In different places, wherever we happened to be. Are they not good?"

"These are all counterfeit," muttered Gostinski. "Let's

see some more.”

Antony grew white. He handed the doctor another wad. Shumski approached the table, examined the bills, and laughed.

“Nobody but a blind man would take such bills. You can paper the walls of your bedroom with them.”

But Antony did not hear the sarcastic words. Ashen-pale, he was looking at the doctor, who did not count the second package but only looked at it, threw it on the table, and said:

“Let’s see more!”

It was the same thing over again. A deep silence fell in the room. The doctor grew more gloomy, stretched out his hand for the money, took it, examined it, and threw it aside. Antony’s forehead shone with cold perspiration. He emptied the bag and looked at it with glassy eyes. Miss Marya put the copper in the safe. Shumski hurriedly walked to the other side of the room. Finally, the doctor laid the last two packages aside and said:

“Only two hundred roubles are good. All the others are counterfeit. You have done a splendid business.”

“How can it be?” whispered Antony.

“If you don’t believe it, you can take them,” said the doctor, pushing the pile of notes toward Antony.

“I told you how it would be,” said Shumski. “I told you to send Shishko, but you had no confidence in my advice.” Then, turning to Antony, he said, smiling:

“Well, sir, this is worth a little more than the few oxen whose skins you brought this winter.”

“I can see no joy or consolation in remembering the old losses,” said Miss Marya. “Then you were guilty. Today Mr. Mrozovetski is. Anyone is liable to make a mistake.”

“It seems to me that I have lost my mind,” said Antony. “I took this money in the presence of other people, in broad daylight, and I never was drunk. I inspected every banknote carefully, just as you had taught me. None of us saw anything suspicious.”

“It’s the best proof that you are all idiots, and you are

responsible for all of them.”

“My Lord, my Lord!” whispered the boy, clasping his head in his hands.

The doctor rose, walked about the room several times, and then sat down again.

“Well, let us finish this beautiful account. Five hundred roubles in cash; the cost of the caravan is five hundred roubles; and this waste paper stands for thirteen hundred roubles; so there remains for me seven hundred roubles, out of which I must pay you for your work. Take your hundred and fifty roubles. I will pay the others tomorrow.”

Antony had risen.

“When misfortune will take a man, what can he do? I don’t understand what has happened. I took good money, and if I was not cheated with the gold and skins, I don’t see how anyone could have cheated me with the notes. Only one thing could have happened: someone has switched the money, although I swear before God Almighty that I never let hold of the bag.

“You say that I am an idiot and that I am responsible for the loss. And you are right: I am. But then don’t dishonor me by offering me my pay. You know well that I will not take the money. Have pity on me, and permit me by hard work to repay you for the loss. I will serve you until my dying day, and you shall pay me with that waste paper I had brought you. Perhaps I shall be able to pay off my debt before I die.”

The doctor studied him.

The lad was almost weeping, losing control of himself with grief and disappointment. He saw himself humiliated, guilty, and powerless in the face of misfortune that persecuted him so bitterly. He staggered and leaned against the wall.

“My Lord! My Lord!” he said again. “Why did I come here? Why?”

Miss Marya approached her father.

“Father, speak to him,” she said softly. “If you repulse

him, we shall have his life on our conscience. He has been tried by one misfortune after another."

"I don't need your advice," growled the doctor. "Only take that man Shumski away. He irritates me continually. It is evident that someone has stolen the lad's money. We must keep quiet about it. We shall discover the truth sooner or later."

The young girl summoned Shumski. He began to talk, gesticulating excitedly.

"Such incidents as this prove my views. Your father is too old for business. He is influenced by false sympathies. He takes idiots into his service. Today a couple of thousands are lost, and tomorrow it will be ten thousand, and soon his whole fortune will be gone. I would swear that this rascal, in partnership with Czyż or the others, has stolen this money. It is impossible to be stupid enough to believe in his innocence. And it is evident that there is some woman in the case—and I will find out about it."

Miss Marya listened to this tirade indifferently and answered quietly:

"Everything will come to light in time. As to the losses, we will bear them philosophically."

Behind the closed doors, a different conversation took place. The old man put the money in the safe and summoned Antony.

"Come here. You must swear to me two things; first, that you will say not a word about this misadventure. This is necessary on account of my credit and also to aid us in discovering the thief—because it is clear that that money was stolen from you. You must go over everything that has happened in your mind: perhaps you will remember something, some clue. You must also swear that from today, you will obey me absolutely."

"I swear it to you, sir."

"I now take you into my service. You will come here tomorrow, and according to your wish, I will pay you for your service with the counterfeit money you had brought me, except what you need for your necessary life expenses. You will do what I tell you to do. How long it will be, we shall see. Perhaps it will be for your whole life, as you said."

"Very well, sir, my life is not worth much anyway."

"Anything can happen, and everything is still open before you. Remember then that now you belong to me. I will not permit any disobedience. You tried to be independent, and you see what came out of it. Now you will obey me and learn your work from A.B.C."

The young man assented with a nod. At that moment, nothing could move or frighten him: his misfortune had stunned him.

"Now, go and rest. I will tell Shumski to be silent about this if it is at all possible."

The young man left the house like an automaton. He dared not look anyone in the face. Like a wounded animal, he retreated to his den, and there he wept. Now he was buried alive in Siberia, without any chance of ever going back to his native country or ever rising from his misery.

CHAPTER VIII
The Fateful Fistfight

SHUMSKI was a braggart and an egotist but an intelligent one, energetic, and very polished. Thrown without means on the Siberian soil, where thousands like himself had perished, he succeeded in a very short time in gaining a good position. Shishkin disliked him, so he tried to win over the old man's sons-in-law, and in this, he succeeded. With the dissipated Smolin, he was dissipated; with the sharper Berezin, he was a sharper; and he often astonished his friend by the daring he displayed in transacting crooked business, where everything depended on cheek. With daring and cheek, he gambled with and robbed the drunken Smolin and covered his ignorance of his professed profession by a plentiful supply of words gathered from different handbooks and encyclopedias, flooding old Shishkin with a deluge of technospeak whenever an accident occurred at the distilleries. And in time, he became acquainted with all the secrets of the firm and became its specialist in slippery cases.

He had time for everything and was everywhere. Today, he was in the distilleries; tomorrow, by the vodka wholesalers; the day after, in Lebiazha. He knew well how to speculate for his own benefit with old Shishkin's money, borrowing it secretly from the safe and always returning it in time. He could spend the night in dissipation and work the next day as well as though he had slept the night through. He could sing, play, and dance and was the soul of every social gathering. He could adapt himself to any environment and every situation. He also had no principles, no fancies, no bad humors. Everyone liked him, but he had not a single friend.

He ruled Smolin completely. Smolin was a feeble-minded man, and prosperity had turned his mind. Wealth had come to him suddenly after many years of hard work and misery, and he had neither the strength nor the ability to retain it. Shumski shared in all his pleasures and was, at the same time, his tutor and companion. Their proceedings aroused the indignation of the whole village, but their social position was unassailable.

Shumski had a large income and was lucky in all his undertakings. He would have been rich had it not been for his continual gambling.

The cards were fickle: what he won from Smolin, he lost to other gamblers at the club. There, a whole pack of gamblers made their living off him. Consequently, he was sometimes seized with fits of rage and despair and would count the days and even the hours that must elapse before he could leave Siberia.

His antipathy for Mrozovetski was instinctive. He hated him from the first moment they met, and every day he despised him more. Mrozovetski was, to him, not only a foe but a rival— a rival with Shishkin and with the Gostinskis, and especially with the latter, over whom he wished to rule but could not. Antony's misfortune filled him with delight, but it did not satisfy him. It was not nearly complete.

Despite his misfortune, the boy was not lost. He served the doctor, became his friend, and a member of his household. Shumski felt that the ground was slipping from beneath his feet at Lebiazha. And when mechanical difficulties arose at the distilleries, Shishkin would say, with the simplicity of an executioner:

"No matter! If you can't do it, I'll send to the doctor and ask him to lend me his engineer. He has only to look at it once, and he knows immediately what to do."

At such times, Shumski would turn green with rage and swear vengeance in his soul. But one day, Mrs. Smolin added fuel to the fire:

"The doctor's clerk was here today," she said, addressing Shumski. "He's a very nice-looking boy and so kind and thoughtful. Miss Marya will be stupid if she does not trade you for him."

These words drove Shumski straight to Lebiazha. It was dusk when he arrived, and the family was gathered in the doctor's room. The doctor was playing whist with three old men from the village. Mrs. Utovich had just replenished the fire, and Andukaytis was silently watching the fire and crumbling some stale old bread. Mrozovetski played the violin, and Marya listened, her head resting against the wall.

Shumski's entrance startled them. Mrs. Utovich hastened to prepare the supper, Andukaytis muttered something about fetching wood for the fire, and Antony set aside his violin. Marya alone did not move. Shumski greeted the company, exchanged a few witty words with the whist players, and then approached his fiancee.

"I have interrupted a pleasant entertainment," he said sarcastically.

"Not at all. We can continue."

"And if I object?"

"We will consult your taste. From whence does the Good Lord bring you?"

"From Kurhan. This is the first time in my life that I have seen you doing nothing but daydreaming."

A movement of the eyebrow was her only answer.

Mrozovetski left the room, not wishing to eavesdrop on their conversation. Shumski followed him with his eyes.

"I was told today in Kurhan that he had replaced me in your favors," he said suddenly.

"Who told you this? Mrs. Smolin?"

"You guessed well."

"It is not difficult to guess. One recognizes the author by his style. What more did she say?"

"Nothing. That was enough for me."

"She was very kind not to say anything more."

"Then you affirm this?" he asked sharply.

"I?" replied she just as sharply. "You know that if it were so, I should be the first to tell you."

"You have no right to speak or act as you do."

"Nor have you, and—"

"Then you believe the stories that man tells of me?"

"Mr. Mrozovetski has never said a word to me about you. It would be superfluous."

Having said this, she rose and left him.

Shumski suddenly realized that this splendid match was at risk of slipping from his grasp. He would have to be more careful now. After the guests departed, he ate the supper that had been prepared for him.

"Boys," called the doctor, "go to bed. At daybreak, Andukaytis will go to Gladianka for grain, and you, Antony, will make vodka deliveries."

They were sitting near the stove and answered together: "Yes, sir."

After a while, Mrozovetski elbowed the Samogitian:

"Will you exchange assignments with me?" he said in a whisper.

Andukaytis opened his wolf-like jaw and laughed in his lazy fashion.

"You wish to go to the *futor*," he answered in a low whisper. "Very well. I will."

But Shumski overheard the whisper and remembered it.

The following day, Antony went to fetch the grain. On

his way back, he went ahead of the wagon and turned into the steppe to the shaman's farm, and only toward evening, caught up with the driver near Lebiazha. He had done this several times—every time a trip took him in that direction—and he had always managed it without attracting any attention. That evening he was in gay spirits as he entered the house. He was surprised to see Shumski.

"Why so late?" asked the doctor.

Antony noticed that everyone looked at him inquisitively. Even Miss Marya raised her eyes from her book.

"I did not think I took longer than usual," he answered.

"Why did you switch assignments with Andukaytis?"

"I thought it was immaterial to you who made the delivery as long as all was in order."

"Well, yes. But did you not stop anywhere along the way?"

The boy hesitated a while. He wished to tell the truth, but he feared that the doctor would forbid future visits to the *futor*, so he muttered:

"No, sir," and blushed in shame.

Shumski laughed triumphantly.

"Why make such a secret of your visit to the shaman? It's natural that one should remember to attend to his own business. One must see his partner and ask him what interest the thirteen hundred roubles bring and then about his daughter's health. Time flies agreeably at the fireplace of the family. Yes?"

Mrozovetski dropped his eyes before the stern looks of the doctor and his daughter, but he could not bear the insult and irony.

"It is none of your business, Mr. Shumski," he said, pale with anger. "I have the right to have my acquaintances, provided I do not neglect my duties. If I had stolen the money, I would not be working here to pay it back but should lead a high life like you."

If Shumski had not been there, perhaps he would not

have lied and would not have gotten angry. But getting angry made his position worse.

"Then you went to see the shaman?" asked the doctor, drumming on the table with his fingers.

"Yes, sir," he answered laconically.

"Do you go there often?"

"As often as I can."

"You have a sweetheart there?"

This inquiry and Shumski's snigger angered him even more.

"I do," he answered boldly.

Not another word was spoken to him the whole evening. Shumski whispered ostentatiously to the doctor, Mrs. Utovich sighed, and Miss Marya would not look at him. He felt as though at a pillory. He did not touch the supper, but road-weary and hungry, he went to his room—

the room which had formerly belonged to his friend. He was so angry that his teeth chattered as though in a paroxysm of fever. He could not keep still and walked the room like a wild beast in a cage.

It was very late when Andukaytis entered. Antony stopped walking.

"Shumski has made a thief of me," he muttered. "You have heard?"

"Yes. He has persuaded them, and they do not doubt it anymore."

"A snake!" muttered the boy. "I will repay him one day."

"He is not fit to live," affirmed the Samogitian. He sat down in the corner and was silent for a while. Then he said:

"I think I will escape from here. The old aunt watches me eat as though she would say that I eat too much. I will wait until the end of the winter and then go."

"Where to?" asked Antony.

"To a gold mine. Last fall, a man came here from the mines, and he could not spend what he had brought with him."

"Who is he?"

"A red-headed Shishko. Have you not seen him in Kurhan?"

"Shishko? Franek?" asked Antony, rising suddenly.

"Maybe."

"He must be my girl's brother."

"Are you coming with me to the mines?" asked Andukaytis.

"Are you joking? I am a slave here. And then—I can't prospect for gold; my luck is just too rotten bad. But come, let us get out of here. I am suffocating. Let's go to a dram shop."

They went out, but then Samogitian smelt fresh bread in the kitchen, which delighted him, and he stayed at home.

Toward morning, Antony returned, still irritated, gloomy, and rebellious. From that day on, there was a cold, mute war between him and the doctor's family. He spoke to no one except when business matters required it, and they ceased to consider him a member of the family. He fulfilled all orders precisely but regarded himself no more than a servant. After work, he disappeared from the house and wandered about all evening and half the night. On holidays, he did not show up at all. He ate with visible restraint and often lived for days on a piece of bread. He mended his clothes and washed his linen. In that way, he needed almost nothing from the doctor.

Shumski now never saw him in Lebiazha, and although the doctor and Miss Marya never mentioned him, he understood that he had crushed his rival forever.

A couple of months passed in this way. Antony was so low-spirited that he had no desire for anything—even to go to the *futor*. But one day, 4escorting a herd of cattle to a distillery, he went to the shaman's little fortress. It was half-covered with snow, as usual, and looked completely deserted. He knocked for a long time, and finally, the owner himself opened the door and said, without inviting him to enter:

"You came to see the girl? Go your way and search for

her elsewhere. She has left me."

"Where is she?" asked Antony.

"Her brother bought her back and took her away. Such was the agreement"

"How long has it been?"

"A couple of weeks. I don't care. In six months, I will get her back even cheaper. He needs her now, so she is nearer to you—in Kurhan. Goodbye," and he closed the door in Antony's face.

Antony sprang into his sleigh and galloped off. He passed the herd and did not even stop in Lebiazha but rushed straight on to Kurhan.

He easily found Shishko's house. It was situated by the Tobol and full of life and light. On entering, Mrozovetski found all the Kurhan gamblers busily at "work." Heaps of banknotes and gold covered the tables, alcohol flowed freely, and the faces of the gamblers were focused on the game.

Mrozovetski asked for the host. He found him at a table with Shumski and several others, all deeply absorbed in the game.

Antony introduced himself to Shishko.

"I am very glad to meet you," muttered the red-headed youth. "Do you wish to play? Pray, be seated. I respect all people who are able to pay cash, drink well, and gamble for three days straight. Sit down with us."

"Thank you. I wish to see your sister," said Antony.

"My sister? You must ask Mr. Shumski. I have promised her to him."

Antony turned to Shumski.

"Are you going to marry Miss Shishko?"

"Is that any of your business?"

"Very much so, for I wish to marry her myself."

"You!" exclaimed Shumski with an insolent laugh.

This was too much for Antony. He raised his arm and struck Shumski in the face.

Shumski fell from his chair but soon was on his feet again, and, seizing a heavy candlestick from the table, he threw it at his assailant. Antony jumped aside and avoided the blow. Shumski sprang at his throat, and a regular dram shop brawl began.

A few gamblers sitting nearby stopped playing to watch the fight but soon resumed their play. The others paid no attention at all. There were so many fights in the place over cheating, counterfeit money, and marked cards: this was just another.

Shishko stared at the two fighting men with bloodshot eyes, whistling through his teeth. Then he took the chalk, changed the figures in the accounts, and took a handful of Shumski's money, putting it on his own pile. Finally, he rose and staggered to a table with several bottles of vodka.

At that moment, Shumski fell, groaning to the floor, and Mrozovetski looked around the place, spat, and went out.

In a few moments, he calmed down and recovered his usual clear judgment. All his love for the girl seemed to have left him; the hideous environment which he had just left filled him with disgust. He entered the sleigh and drove away quickly. Only now, he remembered his duty—the oxen—and the doctor's displeasure, and he drove his horses at full speed until he reached the herd. He overtook it, and for the first time since the summer, he felt free and happy. He delivered the cattle to the over-seers of the distilleries, and in three days, he returned to Lebiazha.

Entering the house, he encountered morose faces. Mrs. Utovich was crying. They looked at him as though they had not expected him back. This terrified him again, and he became sad and silent.

After supper, the doctor called Mrozovetski into his office and closed the door. The boy shivered as though with ague.

"You know Shumski is in bed very ill?" said the doctor.

"I went to take care of him. He is badly hurt. Did you wish to kill him?"

"He has already killed me," muttered Antony. "Had I taken his life, it would not compensate me for the wrongs I have endured from him."

"You are mistaken. Being in the right does not need such proofs. And then, you did not fight over some wrongs but over a girl. So now we must part. After this, I cannot keep you any longer. It would be an insult to the man who is to be my son-in-law."

"But how shall I be able to pay you back my debt? You must not do me this wrong," said Mrozovetski.

"It is your fault, but you have exhausted my patience. Now you may go. I·do not care for your debt."

The boy drew himself up proudly.

"It shall be as you wish. You have no pity on me, and I shall go from here stripped of everything. But the truth does not perish, and the time will come when you will regret this moment. Goodbye."

And so, for the second time, he left Gostinskis' house.

This time he went out boldly.

He went to the kitchen where Miss Marya was alone. He was surprised to see that there was no anger in her face.

"So that man has finally succeeded in ousting you?" she said. "Don't be angry with my father. He was obliged to act in this way. You should not let yourself be carried away by anger. They were not sober, and you were angered by the loss of your sweetheart. You will find her again."

"I shall not search for her. She is as good as dead to me now."

"As is Mr. Shumski to me. I have notified him of that fact by letter."

"Have you parted with him?"

"Yes. Are you surprised? My father is indignant with you and me and him. Where are you going now?"

Instead of answering, he looked at her in surprise that someone should take·the trouble to inquire what was to become of him.

"Don't you think me a thief?" he asked.

"I thought someone had stolen the money from you, and I am sure the shaman did it through the girl. You did not act wisely, and I shall never forgive you for the last few months of anger. You have not rewarded my father for his kind heart."

"The shaman has stolen the money?" he muttered, struck with the thought.

"One day, the truth will come to light. Justice will catch up with that thief one day. In the meantime, you had best follow my advice. Don't go to Andryanek, nor anywhere else, but to old Marcinova Shivitska, the widow who lives alone, with no one to look after her. She was here today, complaining about her hard lot, and I promised to send you there."

The boy seized her hand and kissed it silently.

"Why are you thanking me? This is no favor."

"I thank you for your kindness, I am not accustomed to it, so I am thankful. I have all along supposed that you, with the others, were thinking ill of me, and now I see that you take a note of what becomes of me."

She smiled.

"It's only right. Life has not caressed me either. I am very sorry for you. Now, in farewell, I beg of you to forget all the evil I have done you and remember only the good moments. I hope I shall see you again."

She shook hands with him, and he went into the hall.

She called him back again.

"Take this bundle with you for Marcinova, and greet her for me."

She gave him a large package and held back Tomoy from following him.

From the light and warmth of the house, he went forth into the darkness and cold, but he was so accustomed to this lot that he did not despair. He passed slowly down the street and knocked at the door of another house.

An old woman opened it. It was hardly warmer in the house than out of doors and not much lighter either.

"Miss Marya sent me to you," he said simply, feeling that this time at least, he was not asking a favor.

"Thank God, you have come," answered the woman. "Maybe you will chop some wood for me and fetch me something to eat? For that, I will wash your linen, mend your clothing, and prepare our meals. I can't pay you anything, remember, so you mustn't even think of it."

"I know. Miss Marya told me that. Here is a package from her."

"How kind she is. Let me look inside. Well, well, some lard, some flour, some tea, and sugar. My Lord, if I had some firewood, I should have something for my supper. But I haven't any," she sighed.

"Do you have an axe? I will go to the neighbor, and he will let me have some wood."

"You want an axe? Well, I haven't got one. I gather brushwood for fire."

"Then perhaps you haven't a kettle either?"

"And what kind of a housekeeper should I be without a kettle? I have two."

He began to laugh. He felt at home with this poverty. He looked around the room.

"Is this your house?" he asked.

"Mine. My late husband left it to me. He was a shoemaker from Warsaw. And he wasn't a drunkard, I promise you that."

"You have a rifle?" he said, taking an old rusty gun from the wall

"For heaven's sake," she said, "leave it alone! It might go off!"

"But how? It isn't loaded."

"No matter. It's too easy to have some silly accident, even with an unloaded gun. It might kill someone."

"It will give us bread and butter, not death. With this rifle, I can earn a living," he exclaimed joyfully. "I will bring you some wood right away."

"Wait, wait! I have no water."

"Give me a pitcher, and I will bring you some water."

"One can see that you come from rich people. A pitcher! I fetch the water in a pot."

"Let it be a pot then," he laughed.

Going to a neighboring peasant's to borrow firewood, he thought of Miss Marya with gratitude. He liked his new situation, and he felt that he would be happy there. In an hour, a bright fire shone in the stove, the water was boiling in the kettle, and the old woman trotted joyfully about.

"People passing in the street will wonder at the feast in my house. Marcinova will feast today! Marcinova will be warm today!" she said. "May God give good health to Miss Marya that she let me have her boy."

"You are talking nonsense," growled Antony, busily cleaning the rifle.

"Well, they say you will marry her as soon as she gets rid of that red-headed man. That's why they sent you away for a while until everything is straightened out, and a priest comes. You can't hide anything from me. I know the girl likes you. I have known it for a long time, and when I asked her, she did not deny it. Only that red-headed man was in her way. Therefore she was silent, and you were silent. Well, it·is necessary for a certain length of time to pass and for us to keep quiet about it."

"Are you mocking me?" exclaimed Antony indignantly.

"I am not mocking you at all, but what I see, I see. I go to the store every day for a chat. Sometimes I even buy something. There, I heard her give orders to the cook. 'Keep the dinner warm for Mr. Antony,' and when you were sometimes late, she at once became uneasy and kept looking out the window. And today, she came to me and said, 'Mother, take our boarder into your house. He will take good care of you, and in return, you will look after the poor boy. He must leave our house, and it would be too bad to let him go to strangers.' I said then, 'My precious, I will take good care of your boy. You shall take him as though from his mother's house when the time comes.'"

"And I am sure she told you that you have lost your mind," said Antony.

"She never plays pretend—how could she with me? I'd see right through her. She said nothing but only blushed a little, exactly as you do now."

Antony shrugged his shoulders and fell silent. The old woman served supper.

"Oh!" she said, "I have not eaten anything warm for a week. This smells good."

He watched her and felt sincere pity for the old woman. He was overcome with the desire to provide a warm meal for her every day. Her sallow cheeks flushed as she ate, and her grey eyes shone with delight.

"Now I am full," she said, at last, laying aside her spoon.

Antony did not eat but continued to clean the rifle. Then he unpacked his bundle and arranged his few possessions for a long winter sojourn in his new house. He fell asleep while the old woman said her prayers.

A couple of weeks later, old Marcinova rushed into the store. In a very proud and solemn manner, she asked for a brick of tea, two pounds of sugar, and a package of tobacco. She was not talkative but clearly waited to be questioned. Having received what she asked for, she paid in cash, and having counted her capital, she asked for some muslin and thread.

Miss Marya, while serving her, noticed her behavior and smiled slightly.

"Well, mother, I see you have come into an inheritance," she said.

"I don't need any inheritance," answered the old woman

proudly. "We have plenty of everything. Three cords of wood in the barn, bread in the cupboard, and meat in the pot. We live well."

The girl laughed still more.

"If Mr. Antony is not very busy, perhaps he will go to distribute vodka for me, as Andukaytis is sick," she said.

"No, no!" said Marcinova. "First of all, he is going with me to Kurhan tomorrow. We have plenty of pelts for sale, and we are going to buy some things for the house. So, mind you, he is not some day laborer to serve as a driver with somebody else's horses. Finally, I will not let him go in such cold weather. I am afraid he will get sick."

"Why don't you let him at least come to us on Sundays for prayers?"

"Oh, I should be ashamed to let him go among other people with his ragged clothing. When he is decently dressed, he will come."

"But you let him go to the dram shop every day," said the young girl to rile the old woman.

Marcinova grew red.

"It's not true. It's only bad gossip. He comes in very late from the steppe, and before he prepares the pelts, it is already late. He does not go out at all. Oho! Such an educated gentleman, what should he do in a bar room?"

Miss Marya measured out the cotton. Marcinova paid for it and hastened home.

In the evening, Antony walked over to the doctor's store to buy shot. A feeling of uncertainty seized him as he reached the gate, and he thought about turning back, but overcoming the urge, he entered.

Miss Marya had not expected to see him, and her surprise was clearly visible. He stood to the side, waiting his turn to be served because the store was full of people. At length, he approached the counter and, placing silver money on it, asked for shot without raising his eyes to her. His embarrassment

144

seemed to communicate itself to her, for she did not utter a word, either.

He took the package and turned to go. He raised his eyes as he did so, intending to say goodbye, but, meeting her glance, he blushed and remained silent. She smiled at him but likewise did not speak, and he walked out.

At that moment, both remembered the night when she had found him on the steppe, and though no word had been spoken between them, they felt they had been drawn nearer to each other somehow by that simple exchange of glances.

CHAPTER IX
The Millstones of Justice

ON the first of June, Shumski's contract expired. He sent off his baggage about the middle of May and, during the last two weeks of May, paid visits and settled various small affairs. In the evenings, he played cards at the club. But his good fortune had deserted him, and he lost every day. He was also seen entering Smolin's house every other day. He and Smolin would then confer about something in the latter's office behind a closed door, and when they left it, both seemed agitated. For some time, Smolin had appeared very gloomy and worried about something. Their caravans had already gone into the steppe, but he and Berezin still lingered in town.

Saturday, two days before the time fixed for Shumski's departure, he had a talk with Smolin, after which he went directly to see Shishko.

" I am going away the day after tomorrow," he said.

"Pity I haven't had the time to win all your money from you," rejoined his gambling companion, laughing.

"Oho! You think I am going away poor? I can assure you my pocketbook is well loaded."

"Just don't leave the girl behind."

"And what can you give her for dowry?"

"Dowry? I expect you to pay me."

"Not a kopek."

"You said that if she proved faithful, you would take her with you."

"Oh, I said it because that was the fitting thing to say at the time. You can give her to Mrozovetski now. I hear he is doing well. They say he takes my old place with Shishkin."

"He will take your place at Lebiazha, too. They are only waiting for your departure. You took my sister from him, so now he will marry Miss Marya. I want a thousand roubles for Zosha and demand that you first marry her here, in Tobolsk, before you take her."

"Oh, so now you will tell me that you care for your sister's good name?"

"I'm not telling you anything. You will do as you are told, willy-nilly."

"We will see about that."

"Yes, we certainly will, you fool."

Shumski made no reply to this but went out, slamming the door behind him.

At noon Berezin gave orders for his troika to be readied. He drove it himself and went to Smolin's house.

"Let us go to the bath-house," he said to his brother-in-law.

Smolin climbed into the troika, and they set off. Outside the city, they looked at each other and shook their heads.

"He is a mad dog," muttered Berezin.

"He will make trouble. We must pay him," whispered Smolin.

"He's a dead man. If he had any sense in his head, he would have said: 'Give me something. We worked together on this.' And that would be right, and we would give him a couple thousand."

"But he wants twenty. And he threatens! We should have never taken him into the business!"

"And how? He discovered the corpse in the tallow[30] all by himself. He told me then that he had put him—the barrel and all—under the ice on the Tobol. Now, he says, he has kept him stashed somewhere so as to have "evidence." And you know? It's possible. He is a damned snake! But it's not like he hadn't been useful. He managed to liquidate the promissory notes fast. I would give him that twenty grand and be done with it. He's leaving. Case closed."

"I will not give him a damn kopek, and you will see, he will keep real silent just the same."

"Don't talk like that,"

"Oho! What have you said to him?"

"I promised to give him the money tomorrow."

"Where?"

"At his house. That's how he wanted it."

"It's all the same. I will go see him tonight. You wait on the Tobol with a boat."

Here Berezin turned the horses round, and they went to the bath-house.

The day passed as usual. Owing to the intense heat, the people hid in their houses, and all the streets of the city were empty. The Tobol was broad and calm and smooth as if it were dead.

Having now nothing more to do, Shumski went out for a stroll. He was certain Smolin would keep his promise, and he felt that he had both him and Berezin in his hand. He was not afraid of their assaulting him in broad daylight and among the people, and, for safety's sake, he intended to spend the night at the club. He felt no remorse for what he had done, for to his way of thinking, it was purely a business matter. But the time of waiting seemed to him very long, much longer than he cared.

---

[30] Tallow: rendered animal fat sold to chemical industry for soap making, candles, lubrication, etc.

148

Towards evening, while walking in one of the deserted streets, he ran into the shaman.

"You got any gold?" he asked.

The fortune-teller looked at him attentively.

"I—do," he whispered.

"Come to my house then, let's see it. Perhaps we can do a deal. But beware that you can't cheat me like you cheated Mrozovetski."

The shaman wrapped himself closely in his *khalat*.

"What, Mrozovetski? I don't know him."

"Don't take me for a fool. You robbed him of the good money and gave him paper of your own make. You did it cleverly. I should like to tell him that before my departure, but if you give me good gold, and sell it cheap, maybe I won't tell him anything."

"I will give you good gold and at a good price no matter what," whispered the shaman. "But I am not stupid, and I am not going to your house alone. Besides, I left the bag in my wagon."

"Where is your wagon?"

"In the steppe, hidden."

"Go and get it, then. I will wait for you here."

"No. Someone might see us here. If you don't want to buy, another will—Shishkin's sons-in-law are usually good for some cash," said the shaman, turning around.

"To the deuce with you! Take me to your wagon then," said Shumski, looking at the sun. "There's plenty of time yet."

"We mustn't go together," said the shaman, glancing around. "I will go ahead. You come out on the levy and watch for my hat among the grass. It's not far."

He walked quickly and, once beyond the city, turned and disappeared among the bush. Only his pointed hat could be seen above the grass. Shumski followed it but without leaving the road. Suddenly, a few people appeared in front of him, and on coming nearer, he found them to be Andryanek, Rudnicki,

Karczewski, and Mrozovetski. They carried wolves which they had shot that night in the steppe. Antony walked last, carrying a bunch of skins and a rifle on his shoulder. Mrozovetski did not say a word as they passed each other.

"Well, well! Don't you recognize your old acquaintances?" said Shumski. "You have become very proud now."

He stopped Antony in the road, evidently trying to pick a quarrel with him. The hunters walked on, and Rudnicki laughed.

"They will have nice goodbye, you will see," he said.

Andryanek looked back. The two men stood facing each other, then they turned aside and were hidden by the bushes.

This was the last anyone had seen of Shumski.

In the evening, he was not seen at the club, and Shishko did not find him at home. Towards evening Berezin asked the gamblers about him, but they had not seen him, either.

In the morning, one and another asked for him, and toward noon it was whispered that he had departed during the night without paying his bills.

Andryanek also wondered where Mrozovetski was, for he had not passed the night at the inn where they all stopped, and nobody had seen him in the square of the marketplace. Toward evening he saw the doctor's troika from Lebiazha and asked Andukaytis, who was driving it:

"Are you alone?"

"Yes. I brought some butter."

"Then we will return together."

"As you say," muttered the Samogitian.

They went homeward. By now, Andryanek was very anxious about Mrozovetski.

"He disappeared like the fog," he said to Andukaytis.

"Who?"

"Antony Stefanovich."

"I saw him this morning."

"Where?"

"On the steppe. I even spoke to him. He told me that he had sold the skins and was going home. He had already taken half a dozen partridges."

"Did he tell you how he and Shumski parted yesterday?"

"Not a word. Did they meet?"

"Yes, they did. As we walked past him by the levy, Shumski stopped him."

Andukaytis laughed and pointed to the right with his whip.

"I met Antony there," he said.

Near the spot was a ravine, over which hovered several hawks. Andryanek looked at them with the eye of a hunter.

"There must be carrion there," he decided.

He took aim at one of the birds. Andukaytis reined in his horses as the shot sped away.

The shot hit one of the hawks, and the wounded bird flapped its wings and fell straight down like a stone into the bush. Andryanek, laughing like a child, jumped from the wagon and rushed after the bird. Soon his pink blouse disappeared in the thicket.

Andukaytis stretched himself out on the hay, awaiting his friend's return. All at once, he heard Andryanek's voice coming from the ravine. He screamed :

"Samog! Samog! Come here, quick! "

A few wagons passing by stopped, and people began to call to each other. Andukaytis jumped down also, and they rushed into the bush.

"What is the matter?" they asked.

"God be with us!" shouted Andryanek. "Someone was killed here. The corpse is here."

The thicket opened beneath the pressure of the curious people pressing around Andryanek. Beside the corpse lay the dead hawk, staining with his blood the white flowers of the meadowsweet.

For a while, nobody spoke. The dead man lay on his face as though his face had been shoved into the mud. The corpse had been covered with grass, and only an accident, such as had just happened, could have led to its discovery.

Andryanek approached first and turned the corpse over. They recognized him by his red beard and his broken eyeglasses.

"Shumski!"

Andryanek and the Samogitian looked at each other and understood each other without speaking a word. The others began to inspect the dead man. Evidently, he had been strangled. There were no signs that any defense had been offered. The assassin had attacked him, unaware, from the back and strangled him like one strangles a tiger. The murder had not been committed there. The dead man had been dragged there and left as prey for hawks, foxes, and vermin.

The steppe devours everything very rapidly. If a Kirgiz finds a dead man, he takes his boots and clothing, the birds pick out his brain and eyes, and the foxes clean his bones during the night, and after a week, even the bones are covered with grass. That is the way in which tramps, escaped criminals, lost hunters, and the like usually perish, but Shumski did not expect to perish like a beast or a social outcast. His mouth was convulsed, and his eyes wide open in panic; his face was blue and swollen. The appearance of the corpse was so horrid that the peasants turned away and spat.

Finally, Andryanek took off his cap and made the sign of the cross several times. Then he nodded to Andukaytis. They picked up the corpse and carried it to the wagon. They drove off, followed by the others, in the direction of Kurhan. The frightened hawks disappeared into the sky. Then they returned, flying nearer the earth, searching for their prey. The bolder ones brushed the meadowsweet bushes with their chests and then rose again. They circled about the place for a while, but finally realizing that they had been cheated of their feast, they flew away.

The ravine at once repopulated. The rabbits and *tarbagans* came out of their hiding places, and the partridges and *galanduks* called to each other, running and flittering about as usual. Everything returned to its usual order.

Three days later, three post wagons stopped before Marcinova's house, and people flocked there from all sides. The poor old woman was half dead with fright on seeing the police, who filled her large room.

"Antony Mrozovetski lives here?" asked the commander of Kurhan.

"Yes, sir, but he is not at home. He is on the steppe with his gun."

"Let me see his clothes. Open his trunk also. We must make a search."

"Holy Jesus and Mary! What have we done?"

The official did not answer. The police searched everything and everywhere but found nothing but order and misery and nothing suspicious. Marcinova went from one to the other, kissing their hands, questioning, begging. None would give her an explanation.

The whole village was now gathered in the street and in the courtyard. Finally, Doctor Gostinski came in, and the poor old woman went to him as to her savior.

"My father, benefactor! What is the matter? What do they want with my Antony?"

"Well, everything points to him as the murderer of Shumski."

"Sweet Jesus! Antony killed the red beard! Great Lord! Who says so? He went out very late today. He will be back soon."

"Be quiet," someone said to her.

"I will not be quiet. What? Can I not defend him? They want to wrong my boy, and am I to let them do it? I will not. He a murderer! You are murderers yourselves! My Lord, My

Lord!" and she began to cry aloud. They wished to carry her off, but she defended herself like a fury, and they could not manage her, so they let her alone.

But soon, Antony entered the house.

"What is the matter here?" he asked in great surprise.

"Oh, Jesus!" screamed Marcinova. "They dare to accuse you of killing the red beard. Do you hear that?"

Mrozovetski became deathly pale and looked around with frightened eyes.

"Kill Shumski?" he repeated. "Is he dead? Dead and still pursuing me? My God, this will never end!"

He dropped his hands and, for a moment, remained motionless. Then, as though awakening from a dream, he passed his hand over his forehead and asked:

"And where is my accuser? Who saw me kill him?"

"Come here and answer," said the commander.

"What were you doing last Saturday and Saturday night?"

"Last Saturday, we went hunting. There were four of us. We killed two wolves and, towards evening, went to Kurhan. I took the pelts there for sale."

"Not far from town, you met Shumski. You remained with him, and from that time, no one saw you for several hours. What were you doing?"

"I remained with Shumski because he stopped me. We talked for about ten minutes."

"Did you quarrel?"

"Yes. We always quarreled."

"And what did you quarrel about this time?"

Antony grew red.

"I cannot repeat it. But seeing that he wished to provoke me, I left him, and he went into the bush. I went direct to Shishko, who had ordered some pelts from me, and, as the night was bright, and I intended to hunt on the way home, I did not go to the inn but set off for home."

"Yes. In the morning, Andukaytis met you. Do you remember what you talked about?"

"I remember. He said: 'I understand that Shumski is going away today.' I answered: 'It will be difficult on account of his different entanglements.'"

"Yes, it is difficult for a dead man to go away," muttered the commander.

Antony sighed profoundly. The blow was so sudden and unexpected that he was practically senseless. He answered like an automaton. He was not sure that it was not all a nightmare, a dreadful dream.

"Why should I kill him?" he said. "Had I wished to kill him, I would have done it when he wronged me every day. Now he was going away and therefore could not wrong me anymore. I had no interest in his death."

"Then you claim you are not guilty?"

"Why should I say that I am guilty? I left him in good health. Now, for the first time, I hear that he is dead."

"You make the matter worse for yourself by denying it. It is very simple. You quarreled, and it ended in a fight. It was not the first fight between you. During the fight, you strangled him and then took the corpse on your shoulders and hid it in the thicket. Everyone knows that you hated each other, and several times you threatened him. Get ready. You must go to Tobolsk. All evidence is against you."

Marcinova roared like a wild beast.

"Why do you take him? Who saw him kill the other? God's thunderbolt will strike you! I will not give him up! I will not let you take him. Prove that he is guilty! Dragging an innocent man into your rotten prison: is there no punishment for you? Antony, speak! Why do you stand there like a tree? Bring your witnesses!"

Mrozovetski went slowly across the room and hung his rifle on the wall. Then he raised his eyes to the two peasants who approached him. One of them was Andryanek,

"Are you to take me away?" he asked sadly. His friend, the hunter, nodded.

"Are we going immediately?"

"Without any delay. Such is the order."

"I am ready then."

The commander had already gone out, and the onlookers began to scatter, having satisfied their curiosity.

Marcinova cried incessantly. Only now, the doctor approached the guards.

"Give him time to breathe and rest. He has been on his feet all day, and he is hungry," he said.

Antony looked at him gloomily.

"I can go," he muttered. "I shall not be hungry long, and my tired feet will now rest in jail."

"Well, don't despair yet. They will soon free you, and you will come back vindicated."

"I don't need to be vindicated because there is no evidence against me. But something's telling me that I shall not be back just the same," answered the young man apathetically.

Finally, he noticed the old woman's groaning. He turned to her and kissed her hand.

"Don't cry, mother. Be in good health. We can't help it; such is my destiny. With God's help, you will find another in my place. Thank you for your kindness to me."

Marcinova did not seem to understand.

"Let us be going," said Andryanek.

Antony went out into the street. There was a blackness before his eyes, and his knees trembled. Taking advantage of the cover of the dusk, he glanced toward the doctor's house. His heart became flooded with bitterness, and he turned around and walked quickly. They passed the village, and the empty road stretched before them, with the blossoming steppe on either side. But Antony would no longer go there to hunt beast and bird. A great sadness seized him. He had possessed only one thing—the property which belongs to everyone, even a poor man—his liberty, and he had loved it. Now he had nothing: nothing to lighten his sad lot.

With his head sunk between his shoulders, he walked on without even feeling tired. He took no account of either his movements or the external world. He only felt that he was approaching some end, that everything in him became stiff, that he was afraid of nothing and desired nothing.

A full moon shone in the heavens, and a great quietude fell over the world. Somewhere in the far distance, the bells of a troika rang out. Andryanek walked ahead of him, and the other guards marched behind him. From time to time, Andryanek stopped and listened. The bell sounded nearer, and finally, they heard the rumbling of an approaching wagon. The horses were walking slowly, and when they were opposite the prisoner, he raised his eyes and stopped.

It was Marya. Evidently, she had heard of his misfortune in Kurhan. She ordered the coachman to stop, alighted from the wagon, and approached the men. Andryanek greeted her.

"What a misfortune!" he said. "Could I have foreseen it that I should be obliged to take him in, him, my friend and companion, to prison, I would have feigned illness."

"It is dreadful," she whispered. "What a horrible calamity. Can you not find an alibi? Where were you after you left him?"

"At Shishko's house."

"Very well. I will talk with Shishko about it."

"Don't do that. People will say—God knows what. Pray, leave me to my fate. I was destined to perish."

"It is not true. You will survive this. I am sure of it. Maybe it is the last one before your luck turns. They take you to Tobolsk in stages. What torture! This Shumski was a bad spirit. Why did he stop you then?"

Antony said in a low voice,

"He said that I have stolen you from him, that I was anxious to lay hands on your riches, and that I had robbed him of your dowry. He was—a little unhinged. I neither attacked him nor defended myself but simply looked upon him as a lunatic, and after a few minutes of listening to his harangue, I left him there. I thought to myself: 'You have made me a thief of me, and now you are accusing me of being a scheming rascal. May the Good Lord give you godspeed home, and may we never meet again.' But now—now it seems he has managed to make me a murderer!"

The girl put her hand on his shoulder.

"It is dreadful, but it will pass. It has to. We will take care of you and defend you. Make your mind easy, and be patient. But I see they have taken you away without even letting you take a few things with you. Here is some money. Tomorrow I will send you some clothing. Take it."

"No, thank you," he said, drawing back quickly.

She looked at him.

"Won't you take it?" she said softly. His heart throbbed, and he obeyed her.

"Don't forget Marcinova," he begged.

"No. Don't worry about her. She shall not lack for anything."

"If there is a letter from Valka, and I do not come back from prison, please write to her that I am dead. It will be easier to bear than the truth and probably true in any case."

"You will come back," she said, with conviction in her voice.

He shook his head

"You can't help him now. We must be going," sighed Andryanek.

They shook hands and parted. In Petrofka, other guards took charge of Antony, and thus he walked from village to village, several hundred versts, to Tobolsk.

Near Lebiazha and Kurhan, where he was known, he met with commiseration and was well treated. He rested at the houses of friends, who offered him food and drink. But farther on, where no one knew him, he was to the onlookers, nothing but a murderer: an object of curiosity, aversion, and brutality. At the police stations along the way, they chained him up and fed him on bread and water. On the road, the guards shoved him along and cursed him. The unfortunate man, being tired and badly fed, could not walk as swiftly as the guards and stumbled along, scorched by the sun and parched with thirst. He met with blows and was continually reproached for the murder of Shumski. In that way, he was dragged along for ten days.

Finally, they arrived at Tobolsk, and he rested in prison. He was thrown into a dirty cell to await his turn, and only then did he have time to think.

He thought of his childhood spent with a man who had robbed him. He thought of his education, acquired at the cost of hunger; of his youth wasted in the struggle for bread; of his sister, alone and in poverty; of his fiancee who had died of misery. He thought of his stolen patrimony and of his two years in Siberia, beginning with the theft of all his money, his near-death on the cold steppe, and now this filthy prison. Ill-fortune had tried all her experiments on him, as scientists try their experiments on frogs and rabbits. All courage had left him long ago, and he was resigned to his fate, whatever it might be.

When a whole month passed, and he was not called, he ceased to expect a court proceeding. He doubted even whether the usual sentence of hard labor might ever materialize. He would surely remain in that prison cell and waste there and die. The keepers, who had been very severe with him at first, became more lenient after getting to know him better. Some even took a fancy to him and expressed their doubt that he was a murderer. One day they even permitted him to take a walk in the prison yard. He begged them, as a favor, to be allowed to work on the roads. The work was hard and done by convicts, but it was out of doors, and the food was better, but his request was refused. He might one day be proven innocent and freed, but then again, he might rot in his cell to death.

One day he was summoned before the investigating magistrate. Having heard the accusation, he said nothing but only wept. Everything was against him. In the end, such chaos arose in his mind that he no longer understood whether he was delusional now or had been delusional on the river levy months ago.

"Perhaps you have some witnesses. Who saw you that evening?" asked the judge.

"Shishko saw me immediately after my talk with Shumski. But in truth, only the dead man could be my witness that I have not killed him. It is true that we quarreled. He was jealous of my skill as an engineer, and he regretted losing Miss Marya. But I did not touch him. By the love of god and of my country, I have not!"

"Then we will bring Shishko here. In the meanwhile, maybe you will be able to recall some other circumstances."

The magistrate looked at him with sympathy. The man before him aroused his pity. His thick hair was strewn with silver, and his sad look compelled commiseration.

Another month passed, and then one day, he was called to the room where the prisoners could receive visitors. When he entered, someone hugged him by the neck, and someone else grasped his hands. Dazzled by the light, he stood motionless and confused. Only after a while, he recognized the brown head of Tomoy, Marcinova's wrinkled face, and the dark eyes of Miss Marya. The dog squealed, the old woman cried, and the girl looked at him sadly.

"Shishko is here," she said, sighing.

"For Heaven's sake, Antony. You are looking so poorly," said Marcinova, still weeping.

Then she began to unpack different bundles and take out and put into his hands various dainties.

"Do you know?" said the girl. "We have looked for Shishko for two months, and finally, Marcinova found him. She went over the whole steppe, searching for him. She went as far as the gold mines on foot, and she brought him to Lebiazha.”

“Oh, mother!” whispered Antony, bending to her knees.

“Yes, I did that,” said the old woman. “Your girl said to me, ‘Without Shishko, he is lost!’ So I got hold of my walking stick and went to Kurhan. He was not there, and they told me he had gone to the gold mines. So, I went there. It is not difficult to travel during the summer. Along the way, some people helped me, took me on their wagon, or showed me the way. Nothing bad happened to me; only my feet ached. But they always do anyway. And I found him and begged him to come.”

“No matter about that,” interrupted Miss Marya.

“On the contrary, it does matter! I brought him here! I thought, ‘If he wants a thousand roubles, then I am sure I know somebody to whom Antony is worth more. If not, I will give Shishko my house, and the rest Antony will repay if I can only get him back.’ My boy, my caretaker, my benefactor. How glad I am to see you again. Now I will come every day until you are free.”

“Is it possible that my luck will finally turn? I cannot believe it,” he murmured.

“My father is at the magistrate’s office with Shishko. In Kurhan, the gossip is that the shaman has killed him.”

“The shaman? Why?”

“Well, they say that no money was found on the corpse, and he had been seen to have money with him. And some huntsmen saw the shaman by the levy that day.”

“My God, if only Shishko would tell the truth. I was in his house for three or four hours, and then I went towards the Tobol to take a rest.”

“Don’t worry about that. That scoundrel will tell the truth, or else the doctor will not give him the money,” said Marcinova.

“I forgot to tell you,” said Miss Marya, “that Shishkin is waiting impatiently for you. He wishes to give you Shumski’s position if we can only clear up this miserable business here.

Your luck is turning, I think."

The jailer appeared bearing a paper in his hand and summoned two footmen.

"Take him before the magistrate," he commanded. Antony went with them in good cheer for the first time in months. The women followed him, and the dog snuck into the office with them. Shishko was there with the doctor.

"The case grows more and more entangled, but your friends have the best opinion of you," said the judge. "The Community of Lebiazha takes you under its care on its own cognizance until the time of the trial. For his part, Doctor Gostinski posts a two thousand rouble bond for you. Thus, I am compelled to set you free until the time of your court case. You may go to Lebiazha, but only with the understanding that you will return here when I summon you. I hope that you, on your part, will make all possible effort to prove that you are innocent."

With a trembling hand, Antony signed the undertaking to present himself in Tobolsk whenever he was summoned and then turned to kiss the doctor's hands. He even shook hands with Shishko. He laughed and cried by turns.

They left without an escort and went to a hotel. It seemed to Antony that he had just risen from a severe illness or that he had been raised from the grave.

Marcinova was intoxicated with joy, and there was plenty of talk in the room. Shishko, looking at them, smiled, and his better part stirred within him.

"I am a rascal, a gambler, and a murderer," he said after he'd become a little tipsy. "I have stolen gold, marked cards, and knocked people on the head. And how much counterfeit money have I planted on the Kirgiz! And yet, I am free while this poor fellow has sunk so deep. Whoever iced Shumski, whoever he was, was very clever. I am anxious to know who it was. I will help you find him. I promise you that."

"It was the shaman, I think," affirmed Miss Marya.

162

"This will be a good lesson· for you," said the doctor, slapping Antony on the shoulder. "From now on, you must abandon your night-time wanderings. Well, let us be going. Andukaytis, get the horses ready."

They started home. Antony drove the women, and the Samogitian drove the troika with the doctor and Shishko. It was already cold, and everything around was dead. Marcinova, wrapped in a sheepskin coat, spoke little.

"Are you not cold, Antony?" she asked from time to time.

"No, mother," he answered. "Freedom warms me."

Maybe something else warmed him too: the conversation with Miss Marya.

Marcinova wanted to listen to their conversation, but soon the cold compelled her to draw her ears beneath the furs, so she only shook her head and said:

"I wonder how you can talk through hundreds and hundreds of versts. I should not wonder if you were quarreling, but you are talking so agreeably. What is interesting about that?"

Miss Marya laughed. They passed Kurhan and felt as though they were already home. Antony looked around and reined in the horses.

"I lay here," he whispered, "and I thought it was the end of me. And I had no idea my salvation was so close."

"And then you reproached me bitterly for saving your life. That's gratitude for you."

He bent over, wrapping up her feet solicitously.

"It was on account of Shumski," he answered. "Do you remember that at Petrofka, I wished to give you my last twenty kopeks for the ride?"

"And you—do you remember how you refused to take the *tulub*?"

"And what about your goodbye when I left your house the first time?"

"And your answer when father asked you about that girl?"

"Tomoy alone loved me and trusted me."

"I was betrayed even by him."

"But you like him nevertheless."

"One must like something."

"Did you like Shumski?"

"Much less than you liked Miss Shishko."

He shook his head. They rode on for a while, and then he asked suddenly:

"Do you remember the last time I bought some shot in your store? At that moment, it seemed to me that I was back in my own country. I seemed to smell the lilac and hear the song of the nightingale."

"You were longing for European spring. Now, if you will take the position Shishkin offers you, you will soon be able to return home. One prosperous year and you are free."

"I am not free. I must work and pay back my debt to your father. Perhaps you will learn to like me one day, too. Every man must have something in this world. Perhaps I shall earn that something one day."

The girl smiled silently. The golden cupola of the orthodox church of Lebiazha could already be seen in the distance. Marcinova opened one eye and saw that Antony had already turned his entire back to the horses and faced his two passengers.

"Goodness gracious!" she said. "I am glad we did not have an accident with such a careless driver. I see now that what the people say is true: there is a special Providence which watches over drunkards, children, and lovers."

"You are right, mother," affirmed Antony quietly.

There was a great celebration at the doctor's house that day.

The whole village came to see the released prisoner. The dining room was full of smoke, samovar steam, and noise. They drank an ocean of tea and consumed a mountain of cold cuts. Nobody doubted Antony's innocence.

In the evening, Shishkin arrived. The millionaire spoke familiarly with the peasants, drank tea *na prikusku*—from his saucer, taking first a lump of sugar between his teeth, and, after his tenth glass, he shone with perspiration. There was no difference between him and the others, except that he was fatter, and a bigger pocketbook peeped out from his greasy tulub. He spoke mostly about business and, from time to time, looked at Antony from beneath his heavy eyebrows. Finally, he rose and called the doctor into another room.

"I came to fetch your technician," he said.

Gostinski made a grimace.

"I need him also. Besides, his case is still not finished. I put up two thousand roubles for his bail. He must go to Tobolsk whenever he is called. I don't know if he will be able to satisfy you."

"Casimir Stanislavovich, you are a smart man! You want to keep him for yourself. I will buy his bond, and I will charge you one rouble less on every ox you put in my distilleries. Only give me that young fellow."

"And how much will you pay him?"

"I will give him one hundred roubles a month, room and board, and expenses."

"Vasilii Teodorovich, it is not enough. I will not let you have him for less than one hundred and fifty roubles. But wait, I will call him here."

He went into the other room and saw Antony and Miss Marya talking quietly.

"Listen," he said. "Shishkin wants you. I have asked a high price for you. Do not come down from that price because you will have plenty to do there, and, besides you, there is no man fit to take the position in the whole county."

"Perhaps I shall not be able to fulfill all the duties of the position."

"You must. It's your future. You paid enough for your tuition. Now it's time you had some benefit from it."

"If only Smolin and Berezin leave him alone," said Miss Marya. "He is not Shumski, who got along by flattering them."

"Well, he must keep in with the old man."

He returned to the office with Antony. After an hour's talk, the young man had accepted the new appointment and left the room completely intoxicated by the unusual prosperity which had suddenly come into his life. Laughing delightedly, he showed Miss Marya the agreement and a month's salary, which he had been paid in advance.

"Every month, I shall pay your father a part of what I owe him—if only this Shumski will stop tormenting me."

"They say that a victim's blood cries for revenge and finds the murderer. His murderer must come to light."

"During the three months in prison, it seemed to me that nearly every evening, he stood in the corner of the cell and mockingly repeated, *anima vilis! Anima vilis!*"

He passed his hand over his forehead.

"But now I think I shall beat him because there is nothing worse that bad fortune can throw at me."

They talked together, standing near the window, away from the others. By this time, Shishkin had stopped drinking tea and was drinking vodka and rum. He was puffing like a porpoise. Finally, he rose and prepared to go. His small, bloodshot eyes roamed around the room until they espied Antony. He stumbled over to him and, leaning against him, said:

"Let us be going, my soul."

"Better stay overnight. It is very cold," said the girl.

"Cold is good for you! Cold makes you virile!" laughed the old man. "Well, Marya Kazimierovna, you must part with your boy. I will take him with me. If I had a third daughter to give away, you would never see him again. But you are stronger than I am. Now say goodbye to him and give him some good advice." Here he lowered his voice. "He must treat Smolin like this," and he clenched his fist, "and Berezin like this," making a caressing movement with his hand. "Otherwise, it will be with him as it was with the other man. Nobody would tell him this but me, and I tell him because I wish to keep him for a long time."

The two young people looked at each other in astonishment. Was it a drunken man's vagary, or was he revealing an important insight?

Shishkin said nothing more.

CHAPTER X
Death Comes for the Shaman

THE winter and the summer went by. The Kirgiz had driven millions and millions of sheep to Kurhan, and the dreadful slaughter reddened the ground with blood. The whole Tobol ran red. Batteries of pots melted the tallow,[31] and the streets and squares were lined with steaming barrels. Tens of thousands of animal hides swayed on sticks, drying in the wind. Just beyond the city limits, packs of feral dogs fought over the discarded entrails, and the people could hardly move after the day's hard work. The steppe was covered with Jack Frost, and the Kirgiz were readying to drive their herds toward the south, loading their yurts on their horses and setting out for their winter pastures.

One day, a young woman alighted from the post coach and entered the square. Everyone was so busy with the butchery that no one noticed her. She looked around at the half-wild crowd and nearly retched at the smell of grease and blood. Her ears were filled with the dreadful noise made by the animals and people. Finally, she stopped a man who held a piece of bread dipped in sheep's blood, devouring it ravenously as he walked slowly through the crowd.

---

[31] The production of tallow involves melting animal fat, then straining away any solids.

"Can you show me the way to the house of Mrozovetski?" she asked.

"There, at the corner. I am going there myself. You can follow me."

"And my trunks?"

"Leave them here. I will send a wagon to collect them. But you will not find Antony home. He came yesterday with sheep from the steppe, and he will not be home before all of them are slaughtered. I am going to fetch dinner for him."

"How far away are the sheep?"

"A couple of versts on the Tobol."

"Will you take me there?"

"Sure. Are you perhaps his sister?"

"Yes."

"He will be very glad to see you. When you did not come in the spring, he doubted if you would ever come."

"Perhaps he is already married?"

"They were waiting for you. The whole summer, he was out in the steppe with Berezin's cotton. He brought back twenty thousand sheep. There will be plenty of work for a month."

While talking, they arrived at a very decent-looking stone house. Andukaytis opened the kitchen door and shouted:

"Mother! Antony's sister has arrived. Give her something to eat."

Marcinova welcomed the newcomer with great joy. She seized her face in her hard hands and kissed her on both cheeks. Then she looked the girl over attentively.

"You are not looking well, my dear girl," she said. "I can be proud of my Antony's looks. He must be tired now after his long trip on the steppe, but before he went, he looked like an apple. You glutton, get away from my stove. What do you want?"

"I am hungry," muttered Andukaytis.

"First, I must take care of the girl, and then I will prepare food for my Antony. Then I will feed you. You must wait your turn. And you, young lady, sit down and have something to eat."

"I am anxious to see Antony."

"Of course. Of course. Andukaytis, have the carriage ready. We are not poor, you know, we don't walk like the common people, we take the carriage. In the meantime, I will have your luggage brought here and get your room ready. Glory to God, you have come! The boy needs a woman's hand."

Valka smiled sadly.

In a short while, Andukaytis had the *kibitka*[32] ready, and they set off. Beyond the city limits, all the fields were covered with sheep carcasses, and their horses waded in pools of blood. The people, covered with blood and grease, looked like the souls of the damned. Andukaytis, screaming at the top of his lungs and waiving his whip, made them yield, but sometimes the travelers were obliged to stop and wait, breathing the steaming stench rising from the discarded entrails. Finally, the Samogitian stopped the horses.

"We must walk now," he said. "There is Antony coming."

Valka watched the slaughter of the sheep. Some men killed them, others skinned them, others carried away the offal, and others yet carved the meat and threw it in heaps like firewood. The blood flowed down to the Tobol, and in the stream of gore walked dozens of men, bending beneath the weight of fresh skins. These they placed in a heap in one place, where a fat old fellow counted them and marked their number in a book in inexpertly calligraphed figures. All the people wore worn-out felt boots, pink shirts, dirty coats, and faded caps.

Having just returned from the steppe, they did not care about their appearance. The dust, wind, and perspiration had marked their faces; their hair was long, wild, and greasy, and their eyes feverish from lack of sleep.

---

[32] Kibitka: an enclosed carriage

Valka looked terrified. She could not recognize her brother, and she was ashamed to acknowledge it. She stopped, afraid to walk in the blood splashing about her feet.

Andukaytis rescued her from her embarrassment.

"Antony Stefanovich!" he shouted. "Here, you have your dinner and your sister."

One of the dreadful-looking workers threw his burden from his shoulders and rushed toward them. Only then she recognized something of his features, and, with an impulse of happiness, she threw herself into his arms. Both wept and called each other by name.

A fat peasant approached them.

"Goodday. Be welcome, my young girl," he said familiarly. "You hardly recognized your brother. He is all right."

"Who is he?" asked Valka in a whisper.

"My employer, Shishkin."

The girl opened her eyes wide in utter astonishment. How different things were here from what she had known at home. The people, the country, the customs, the sky even. Everything was different and strange. And powerful.

After the greetings were over and Antony sat down to eat his dinner, she got a better look at him. He did not appear as strange now as he had appeared at first. The strength, the sense of self-worth, the repose, and the hardening and settling of his figure had erased most of his old, boyish characteristics. He was older and heavier. His voice was hard, his looks were sharp, and even his features were sharpened and more pronounced. But it was him: her brother.

While eating and talking with her, he still kept an eye on the business. He watched the number of skins, gave orders, and answered queries of some businessmen. Having refreshed himself, he embraced her once more.

"Now, I must return to my work. You go home and rest, and perhaps toward evening, I will drop in to see you."

"Haven't you somebody else to carry these skins?" she

asked. "Is that proper work for a graduate of an Institute of Technology?"

"Well, things are quite different here, my dear. No one here stands on ceremony. Everyone has two hands for every kind of work. And then, I have some interest here, too. Over twenty thousand sheep are my share of this slaughter. So I better see to the work and to the accounts."

He left her and went back to work.

She returned home and was obliged to be satisfied with the company of Marcinova.

In the house, partly occupied by Antony, there was also Shishkin's office, a warehouse, and a dram shop, which was as full of people as a bee hive. Valka was lost in this labyrinth. She wondered at the disorienting movement and noise.

After a whole day's rest, she found her way to the city and the place where people were still slaughtering sheep. She went there every day for a short chat with her brother, wondering at his incessant work. The rest of the time she spent in the kitchen, trying to be of some help to Marcinova.

One morning, Valka was left alone. Marcinova went to the market, having bidden the girl to bake some bread. Valka had the best of intentions but no experience. However, she began to mix and knead the dough as best as she could imagine. While she was doing this, a young girl entered the kitchen, asked for Marcinova, and, hearing that the old woman was expected soon, remained. She took off her furs, rubbed her cold hands, and behaved as though she was in her own house. A man came in, and they transacted some business. Valka had become accustomed to Siberian informality and did not pay any attention. The young woman, however, started a conversation.

"You don't know how to knead bread," she said, and without hesitation, she rolled up her sleeves, sinking her white hands in the dough.

Valka looked at them and could not refrain from uttering an exclamation: she beheld on the girl's finger her brother's ring.

"Then you are Antony's fiancee!" she exclaimed.

"Yes. And you?"

"I am Valka."

"Valka! He did not tell me of your arrival! When did you come?"

"A week ago."

"A whole week, and he did not tell me anything."

"I have hardly seen him myself."

"Well, such is life here. A beginner wishing to make money must, of necessity, become almost a wild man. We will bake this bread, and then we will go to Lebiazha."

"Thank you, but—" whispered Valka.

Miss Marya smiled.

"You will see him there more often than here," she said, blushing slightly.

Quickly and with experience, she divided and shaped the dough into loaves and put them into the warm stove to rise.

Marcinova arrived.

"Our young lady!" she exclaimed. "Goodness gracious! I will send for Antony immediately."

"He will not come because he will know that I do not wish to disturb him in his work. On the way home, I will go and see him myself. But then I do not have much time either. The store is empty, and the dram shops are without vodka. I must be going. I will take Miss Valerya with me."

The old woman protested but to no avail. The girls attended to the errands together and then started off, Miss Marya driving. Beyond the city, the slaughter was still in progress.

Antony recognized his betrothed from afar and immediately came to see them.

"Oh, God, how horrid he looks!" thought Valka.

"How does he dare show himself to you looking like that?"

But his fiancée smiled at him warmly, and her sun-burned face lighted up with happiness.

"How is our father?" he asked.

"He is well. And what success have you had?"

"I shall clear three hundred roubles."

"How long do you think you will have to work?"

"A couple more weeks."

"Any news about the case?"

"Shishko has disappeared."

"We are waiting for you."

"Thank you for taking Valka with you. As soon as I am through with this work, I will come and spend the whole week with you."

"You had better go back to your sheep now. Goodbye!"

He kissed her hand and looked after her as they drove off.

The girls became better acquainted during the drive. Valka questioned Marya about everything, but mostly about her brother. She then learned the dreadful history of his life in Siberia and wept a little. Then, kissing her companion, she thanked her for the help she had rendered him.

"Without you, he would have been lost hundreds of times. How can we ever repay you for all that?"

"He did more for me than I for him," answered the girl seriously. "I was angry and vindictive and hard. Nobody loved me, and I cared for nobody. He made me better. He taught me how to be happy. He understood my sick soul, and I knew his bad lot. We suffered and fought together. Now we are not afraid because we shall go through life together."

"I thought I should find you already married."

"We are waiting for the end of that horrid case."

"Then you will remain here forever?"

"He must still work here for a long time yet, to make his fortune. But remain? Who remains here if he is not bound? Like the birds, we will await the time of departure. My God, I have already waited so many years!"

A few tears flowed from her eyes.

From that moment, Valka loved her dearly. Soon she loved the whole family and felt as though she was among her own people.

Antony did not put in an appearance for two weeks, and then he had only a few days' leave.

Siberia was already in the grasp of winter. The snow fell, and storms whistled about the house. The evenings passed very pleasantly, spent near the fire in the doctor's room—they never had enough chatting about their country. When Valka spoke of it, all eyes were directed toward her, their cheeks flushed, and their hearts raced. She was seldom interrupted, and when she stopped talking, one could feel the quiet and hear the beating hearts and deep sighs.

The doctor's pipe went out; Miss Marya's normally busy hands lay in her lap; Antony forgot to put wood on the fire; Mrs. Utovich's spinning wheel became silent; and the sober, hard-working people became like children listening to fairy tales; like youth, which is ever forgetful of reality.

Valka had a special talent for talking about her country, and the doctor was the first to fight against the poison of nostalgia which sapped their strength and will. He interrupted her and urged that they should retire. On the third day, he forbade the theme altogether.

"Children," he said, "outside is the steppe, and you must remember we are obliged to stay here for a long time yet. You know how people suffer from homesickness in this country. Do you wish to suffer again from what you have already overcome?"

Antony and Marya shuddered as though the cold wind of the steppe blew over them, and the boy, drooping his head, said to his sister:

"Tell us about the people. Is Burski still alive?"

"No. He died. Vistitski's family now lives in Warsaw."

"And our Promieniev?"

"In the hands of strangers."

"He did not enjoy long that of which he robbed us."

Andukaytis entered the room covered with snow.

"I have seen the priest," he said, out of breath.

"Where? What priest?" asked all at once. "A different one, a new one. He has just arrived. I have seen him in Kurhan. He will stay only two days. Then he must move on as he has only a forty-eight-hour pass. I galloped here to tell you the news. I haven't even eaten anything."

Antony looked at Miss Marya, and she blushed deeply. The doctor laughed.

"We better hurry with the sacraments," he said.

"I am going to see him immediately," said Mrs. Utovich. "Perhaps he knew my brother? Marya, where is your white dress? Miss Valerya, you must fix her veil for her. I am afraid we shall be late!"

She rushed to open the closet and to order Andukaytis. Valka rushed to help her. The doctor looked at the young couple.

"Well, take her, Antony," he said quietly. "I postponed it until we could find a priest. God sends him to us now, and I must give up my daughter. But you must live with me because I could not live alone."

"As you wish, father," whispered Antony, trembling with emotion.

He pressed the girl's hands to his lips.

"I am still poor, and maybe I have not yet deserved this happiness, but you must not refuse now. I ask you to marry me now, today."

"I... accept. And I promise I will make you happy. And myself also."

"Let us get ready then," said the doctor, going out.

The young people were struck dumb for a while. After a time, Antony could contain himself no longer.

"My dearest," he said. "Now, indeed, I am richer than

kings. I thought it would come only after many years, and now that it has come, my heart feels as though it would burst from my bosom."

They went toward the window, standing there awhile, close to each other, forgetting the whole world. Then Marya said:

"I must go."

"Where to, dear?" he asked, astonished.

"To tell the people. We are not the only ones waiting for the priest. Someone must tell them."

"I will send Andukaytis."

"No. No. Good news must be delivered by happy people."

"Then I shall go because I am the happiest."

"Very well. But don't forget anyone."

And now, through the quiet sleeping village, quick footsteps resounded. To some of the houses, a man came, knocked at the blinds, and awakened the poor, sorrowful people. Sleepy, slow voices asked apathetically: "What is it?" with the intonation of those who expect nothing.

And a strong, gay voice answered:

"Hasten, brothers! A priest is in Kurhan, and he will remain for two days only."

Immediately a light shone in the house, and sleep flew from every eye. All hearts beat with joy.

"Sweet Jesus! A priest!" was heard in the voices of men, women, and children.

And the footsteps went further down the street, carrying the good news. Lights shone in the houses, and it grew more lively: the dogs barked, doors squeaked, and people came out into the street.

"Have you heard the news? A priest is in Kurhan."

"Joseph, get the sleigh ready."

"Marysia, wrap up the child well."

"Old man, don't smoke your pipe before confession."

"Kazik, dress for your wedding."

"What shall we give the priest?"

"You must not forget the holy water."

The noise increased. Thus, on a cloudy morning, when the first cock crows, his cry is picked up and repeated further and further until all rise tired and sleepy.

The first sleigh started from the doctor's house. It was followed by a second and a third. The awakened peasants appeared on their thresholds, asking what the matter was, and on being told the news, they returned calmly to bed.[33] Snow squeaked under the sleighs, the forst took the breath away. Dozens of people rushed through the night, as if at a wedding. Carriage bells rang through the night.

In front of the post-station in Kurhan, where the priest stopped, there was a crowd like at a fair and a huge press of people inside. Little children were brought to be baptized, everyone wanted to make a confession. Ten couples were waiting to be married, and everyone pressed around the priest, making offerings, making requests, while he, exhausted by hard work and his journey, staggered, became flushed and pale by turns, but kept up by sheer strength of will. And he was obliged to rush, rush, rush, although all were waiting patiently. Those who had confessed went off to the side and knelt, praying aloud, and awaited the evening mass to take communion. The couples waiting for the marriage ceremony were patient, and even the children did not scream when they were being baptized.

On the second day, when only a few hours in Kurhan remained for the priest, the time came for marriages. There were no banns, there were no processions. The couples followed each other, some had no rings, some stuttered when answering questions. Antony and Marya were the last in line, and when they finished, the priest sang *Veni Creator* for all, but quickly,

---

[33] The local peasants are Orthodox and have their own church and priest

for he still had to sign certificates.

The post-horses were already being harnessed into the post-sleigh, but the priest still spoke about the Egypt of the Pharaohs and the willow trees by the rivers of Babylon where silent lyres hung up rusted away unplayed. He reminded them of the daughter of Jair and the son of the widow of Naim, and, finally, mounting into the sleigh, he raised up his hand and blessed them, praying still as the sleigh started, bore off, became small, and finally disappeared. And the crowd stood there, sending him off with their words, their gazes, and finally, their thoughts.

Antony took his wife and sister in the sleigh to his house in Kurhan. He went to see Shishkin, and the women packed everything in a great hurry. They dined hastily, the doctor constantly urging them to hurry, being probably afraid that unless they left now, his daughter might remain there. Antony obtained a week's leave of absence from Shishkin, and toward evening they drove off in the direction of Lebiazha.

Marcinova and Valka remained in Kurhan, not wishing to bother the young people during their first days together.

In Petrofka, the peasants detained the doctor, begging him on their knees to save them from an outbreak of typhoid fever. He remained there for a couple of days, ordering Andukaytis to bring his medicine box.

And in that way, the newlyweds were left alone, Mrs. Utovich took care of their meals, and their neighbors discretely kept away.

Only toward evening did Mrs. Utovich come upstairs and say:

"There is an unusual person come to the store who wishes to see Mr. Antony."

"I am sure there has been some accident at the distillery," said Antony and went out.

"Who is it?" he asked once they were outside the room.

"Miss Shishko. She said she must see you."

"The deuce! I have no business with her."

"But she has business with you, for she looks very troubled."

He hesitated for a while, then returned to the room.

"The Shishko girl is in the kitchen. Let us go and see what she wants."

They went downstairs. The girl from the *futor* stood in the hall, leaning against the wall. She looked wild and gloomy. She glared at the doctor's daughter like a wild animal and only muttered a greeting.

"What do you wish with me?" asked Antony.

"Perhaps you can tell me where my brother Frank is."

"I haven't seen him since last spring."

"That is bad. He expected to make a pile in this court business of yours, and now he will get nothing. But I don't care for money. I will tell the truth for free. In the spring, Frank told me to return to service with the shaman and keep an eye on the old monster. During the summer, I learned many things which none of you would ever guess. And I waited for Frank. In vain. But yesterday, the old witch brought three robbers to the *futor*. They attacked the old shaman, and before I woke, they stabbed him repeatedly. Hearing the noise and the shouting and groans, I loosed the dogs, seized the rifle, and jumped down into the courtyard, but they all ran away and the old witch with them. The old man is in agony, and what is most incredible—he speaks in our tongue and shouts continually, 'Don't let Mrozovetski in! Bar the doors! Tell him that I am not at home!' I rode here like the devil, and my horse dropped dead at your door. Give me another, for I must go back now. Now you do what you think is right. I have done my part."

"Thank you," said Marya. "Come into the kitchen until they can get your horses ready."

"I don't want to come in," growled the girl.

"Shall I go?" asked Antony, looking at his wife.

"Certainly, but not alone. I am going with you, and we

will also take Andryanek and Lukovski. How far is it to the *futor*?"

"About three hundred versts."

"If only we arrive in time. We must hasten."

A freezing, dreadful night in the limitless steppe was their first wedding night. The sleighs glided over the roadless steppe, directed by the cat-like eyes and hunter's memory of Andryanek. Every twenty or thirty versts, they gave the horses a little rest and bread dipped in vodka, and then they hastened on. The mad ride lasted two nights and a day. When they were only a few versts away, the horses lay down and refused to go further. They left them, rushing on foot the last stretch.

Zosha was first through the gate.

From the hall, they heard an animated conversation, shouting, quarreling, and beseeching.

"Who is there?" asked Antony.

"He is alone. He is talking to himself like that all the while. I wonder he isn't dead yet."

The girl opened the door. A faint light of the breaking day filled the hall, filtering in through the panes of mica. There was great disorder in the hall, for the attack and fight had taken place there. The furniture was overturned and broken, the felt was stained with blood, and various trunks had been broken open.

On a heap of sheepskins, the shaman lay groaning. Although the door made no noise, he noticed and recognized Antony, for he slid back towards the wall, writhing as if trying to hide. Antony drew nearer, the others waited by the door.

The shaman raised his clenched fist and shook it threateningly at Zosha.

"You serpent!" he said. "You brought him here!"

Antony stooped over him.

"Are you afraid of me? Why?"

"O serene and mighty judge!" groaned the shaman, "I served you faithfully."

Then he writhed like a serpent and screamed:

"I don't want to die! I will tell nothing until the day I die! But I am not dying! I will not die! I will live! It's Berezin who sent the murderers. He is afraid of me. But I am not afraid of him. I will tell everything when I die, but not now. Now I will live!"

He covered himself with the furs, but after a while, he came up for air and groaned again:

"God! What is it all worth? I worked so hard, I suffered so much, I carried so much, and now I must die anyway?"

Marya knelt beside the dying man and said: "Shaman! Tell the truth now. No one can drag you into court, but God will call you before His own Tribunal. Mrozovetski came here to forgive you."

"It's not true! Mrozovetski will not pardon me. He is vengeful, and he holds grudges. He will not forgive me. Maybe on his own account, he would, but on account of his children—never!"

"He is talking about my father," whispered Antony. "Who is he?"

The shaman raised his hand and pointed to the corner.

"There! See him? He is waiting there, awaiting my last breath, and then he will seize me by my beard and drag me away. Damned, damned money!"

"He must be... Drozdowski," said Antony.

"You are calling me," whispered the dying man. "Oh, Gryusha, keep quiet. Don't tell anyone. He paid well to use my name. He purchased it. And he gave me as much to give up my tongue. Twenty years without a name! Twenty years without my tongue! And what was it all for? What was it for? Must I die anyway?"

Andryanek and Lukovski came closer.

"Is he one of us?" asked the Pole. "No! I am a shaman!" howled the wounded man.

Andryanek spat on the floor.

"No matter whether you are a shaman or not, it is sure that you are a crook. These thieves took most things from your trunk, but here is Shumski's chain I found. Ah! You black-souled scoundrel, it is because of you that I dragged an innocent man to prison."

The shaman's teeth chattered as though with ague.

"They have taken everything," he growled.

"You stole my money that night and changed it for worthless paper," said Antony.

"No! Not I! The old woman did it. That old witch who killed me. Why did I not strangle her?"

"Drozdowski, what have I ever done to you that you should so wrong me?" said Antony. "Because of you, my father lost his good name, and we have lost our patrimony. Because of you, I have been under suspicion as a murderer and a thief."

"He must now tell us everything," exclaimed Lukovski. "Speak up, you dog!"

"Ha! Ha! Ha!" laughed the shaman. "I will tell you nothing. Why! I shall not go back to where I came from. It is too far. But neither Burski nor Berezin shall say that the shaman did not keep his word. The shaman is like a tomb, like a stone. Who bought him, had him."

"Let us burn the devil!" suggested Andryanek.

Marya overcame her disgust and again bent over the shaman.

"Drozdowski, don't you regret anything? Two orphans were driven from their home because of you. They thought you would defend them, but you—sold them. Now you are dying—and where will you go next? Heaven or hell? But speak up, confess, you may yet be forgiven."

The shaman was silent, his eyes were wide open, and his mouth opened as though to shout.

"Ha!" he whispered. "Those trees, the linden trees, the poplars, the elms. They are coming to get me. They will strangle me. Suffocate me! Judge Mrozovetski's hounds are howling.

Their master is dead. Is dead! And I am also dying. There is no afterlife. We shall never meet."

The shaman fell silent. His hands dropped down and grasped the fur. His head fell backward, his jaw opened wide, and his eyes turned to stone.

"He is dead," muttered Andryanek, spitting. "He said enough. The old woman stole the money. Here is Shumski's chain. We shall find out the rest."

The girl Shishko, standing far off, said:

"You will find nothing. The robbers carried away everything. In the cellar, there were heaps of banknotes. They are there no more. They left only the furs."

"No matter, we will look over the wolf's den," said Andryanek. "What remains Antony will take for his pain."

"I will not take anything. It will leave all for the girl in return for the care she took of him."

They started to search through the *futor*. The fortress was like a foxhole: more underground than above it, and there were dozens of little rooms and closets full of different kinds of merchandise. When they returned to the room where the corpse lay, they looked through all the trunks. Through all their search, they found some gold, some cards, some herbs, old letters, prescriptions, and finally—Shumski's billfold.

"You can remain silent, satan's dog. Here is our witness," said Andryanek, raising the billfold and looking at the corpse.

"We have finished here," said Antony. "Now we must bury him and return home."

"I will not touch him," said the peasant firmly.

"Lukovski, we must do it."

"Not I. I am going to look after the horses."

The girl laughed disdainfully. She took a shovel from a corner and left the house. In a short time, she came back.

"The snow sticks. There will be a storm. We will bury him in the snow for now," she said laconically.

Antony and his wife wrapped the corpse in a piece of felt

and carried it from the hall. The girl preceded them with a shovel on her shoulder. She looked mournful.

She stopped under a birch tree and looked at the two. Her lips moved, and her eyelids quivered. Then she bent down and began to dig in the snow.

Mrozovetski deposited the dead man on the snow and waited until she had finished.

"You spare no pains," said Marya.

"No," she answered, raising her head. "I will make him a comfortable grave in the spring, gather his bones and bury them, and set up a cross. I owe him no less for strangling that bastard Shumski."

Her eyes shone with hatred and gratified vengeance. She looked dreadful and terrifying. A spooky moment of silence followed but then, in the west, the white clouds opened, and the blood-red light of sunset flooded the steppe. And then a cold, whistling wind began to blow close to the ground.

"Buran!"[34] the girl said.

She girl threw aside the shovel and nodded to Antony. They took the corpse and laid it in the snow. Then Marya bent her head and recited the *Angelus*. The girl covered the grave up with snow and then planted the shovel, and looked at the crimson sunset. Antony and his wife were praying.

When they had finished, the girl asked:

"Are you going at once?"

"Yes," Antony answered hastily.

She laughed and went into the house. Lukovski and Andryanek were busy with the horses. They put them in the stable and rubbed them down with vodka, and covered them with felts. Finally, they thought of getting something to eat.

---

[34] Buran is a type of wind which blows across Iran, Central Asia, and Siberia. It takes two forms: in summer, it is a hot, dry wind, whipping up sandstorms; in winter, it is bitterly cold and often accompanied by a blizzard which swirls about and reduces visibility to near zero

The girl opened the pantry and pointed to the samovar, but she herself would touch nothing. She lay down on a bench and, covering her head with a tulub, seemed to sleep.

"We must hurry," said Andryanek. "A blizzard is coming, but it will not catch us before we reach Utyatska."

"It would be better to pass the night here," said Lukovski.

"Here? After such a murder, such a death... I wouldn't stay here it for a heap of gold,'" said the peasant.

Antony looked outside and shrugged his shoulders.

"A blizzard is approaching."

"If we must go, then we had better do so immediately," said Marya.

The men put on their coats and went to get the horses ready.

Marya said to the girl:

"We are going."

"God be with you."

"Will you stay here?"

"Yes. Nobody drives me away from here."

"True. But how will you manage? Will you live here alone?"

"I was always happy here. Only leave me a horse and let me be."

The bells sounded, and Tomoy whined joyfully, glad to return home. Mrozovetski wrapped his wife up solicitously and whistled for the dog, driving off in the wake of Andryanek's sleigh.

The night was clear, and the quiet of the steppe was only disturbed now and then by a gust of freezing wind, blowing very near the ground, at knee height, whirling the snow, then raising a white, cold cloud of dust. And it whistled from time to time.

Andryanek turned, glanced at the sky with the eye of a hunter, then whipped the horses and shouted to Antony:

"Don't loiter behind because if we get separated, the

steppe will devour us."

Antony's troika was excellent. The yellow mare in the center ran remarkably well, and the two side horses, stretching their necks, galloped along. Tomoy could not follow and howled pitifully.

"Antony, let us take the dog into the sleigh," said Marya.

They stopped, and Tomoy jumped in and lay at their feet. But when Antony looked ahead, he could see Andryanek's sleigh no longer. He whipped up the horses and rushed on in the direction from which the bells sounded. They heard the bells—once to the left and then to the right, and he directed the horses accordingly. At length, surprised he could not catch them, he began to listen more attentively, and his heart throbbed.

"I can't make out whether I hear my bell or those of Andryane," he said uneasily.

"Take ours off," advised his wife.

He stopped, took off the bell, and listened. And all he heard was dead silence.

He shouted with all his strength, but his voice was lost in the howling wind without any echo. The air became thick and filled with big white flakes, falling slowly. In a moment, their clothing was white.

"The blizzard," whispered Marya, looking around.

They looked at each other, each seized with a dreadful thought.

"Sit down and let the horses direct us. Hurry them on, don't let them stop, but don't try to direct them. Let them go where they wish."

He obeyed, and they started off.

Darkness fell quickly. The steppe and sky became one grey-white mass, cut with zig-zags of snow, which covered up what little living vegetation remained.

"This is your first blizzard, I think," said Marya. "A few

years ago, I was lost for twenty-four hours between Petrofka and Lebiazha. Father went to search for me with three dozen sleighs, and they found me half dead."

"Here, only God can find us and lead us, for there are no human beings around. Andryanek must have lost his way also."

"Yes. It is difficult to find the way in good weather, and now it is impossible. Don't force the horses but don't let them stop. If they stop, the snow will bury us."

Covered with perspiration, the horses went on, led by the yellow mare, who seemed to know the danger. With her instinct, born of a long life in the steppe, she sniffed the air and earth and became uneasy. The snow was already knee-high. Antony rang the bell and shouted again, but the sound was lost, melted in the thick air. They advanced slowly, unable to see the horses in front of them.

"And there is a chance that it will last three days and three nights," muttered Mrozovetski.

"Yes."

"And when the horses stop?"

"Then—we die."

They looked at each other.

"Are you afraid?" she asked, with white lips.

"My Lord! To die now!" he whispered, shuddering.

"Don't let the horses stop. They must keep moving. They must!" she said.

The sleigh hit something hard: it was a birch stump.

"Woods!" said Antony. "Perhaps it will be better to remain among the trees."

"No, no! Go! Move on! If we stop, we are lost."

He whipped the horses, and they walked on through the snow, snorting, afraid, tired. The sleigh drowned in the snow. At that moment, they heard a whirring noise as though great birds were making ready to fly, and the wind struck the horses in the breast with such impetus that they turned, bent their heads, and staggered as though drunk.

"Buran!" whispered Marya.

The wind drowned their voices. The snow did not fall anymore. Individual snowflakes have disappeared, and only a thick, white fine dust of ice, as thick as milk, flew in the air with great force, whistling, howling, laughing, weeping. This was the wild music of the steppe.

Exhausted and wild with fright, the horses struggled to advance, urged on by Antony's whip, and sinking deeper and deeper in the piles of snow. They moved jerkily, now buffeted by the wind from one side, now pushed on from the back. At one point, Antony looked back at his wife. Her eyes were closed.

"Marya, are you cold?" he shouted through the howling wind. She awakened and stretched herself. "No. Only I am very sleepy."

"For God's sake, don't sleep. You will freeze to death if you sleep!"

"I know it, but I can't resist it."

"Have pity! It is death!"

He paid no more attention to the horses but began to rub her hands and eyes with snow and, finally, to shake her. She came to her senses for a while but soon again closed her eyes. She could not resist further. He forced some vodka down her throat and drank some himself. He felt as though he were turning into a lump of ice.

The horses stopped. The snow reached up to their chests, and in their fright, they began to jump, kick, bite, and neigh, trying to free themselves from the harness. Finally, the yellow mare broke her collar, and with a streaming mane and tail and bloodshot eyes, she disappeared in the blizzard. The other horses, not so strong, neighed pitifully, reared, and finally fell, shuddering and kicking.

Then Antony saw death before him. She stood right there before them, and the snow covering them was her veil, the wind her song. Her domain was this grey-white dust which surrounded them on all sides.

He jumped from the sleigh and took his wife in his arms. He did not know what he was doing. The dog seized him by the sleeve and howled. He also howled like a wild beast. He began to remove the snow from the sleigh and placed the sleeping woman at the bottom, covering her with everything he could find. Then he laid down beside her, warming her with his respiration. Tomoy slipped in and lay beside his mistress.

The snow began to cover this mound, formed by two people, a dog, and a pile of furs. Mortal sleep descended on them. At first, the horses' heads could still be made out against the snow, and there was a feeble movement beneath the furs in the sleigh, the only proof that life still remained. Then, on the level steppe, the horses, the sleigh, and the people formed a hillock that looked like a grave and was as still as the grave. The *buran* grew stronger, and the night seemed endless.

Andryanek and Lukovski had lost their bell. Then the intelligent peasant turned his horses back, and by closely following their tracks, they managed to return to the *futor*. He expected to find Mrozovetski already there and was very troubled at not finding his friend.

"They have lost their way. May the good God save them!" he said, knowing full well that it would be impossible to search for them until the storm was over.

They were very tired and lay down, falling asleep at once. Zosha said nothing to them, pretending to be asleep. But when she was sure that they would not hear her, she rose and, leaning against the window, listened to the storm. She was not frightened. On the contrary, it gave her a wild sort of pleasure. In her mind, she could see the two lost passengers. For one of them, she would willingly have given her life, the other, she could have killed with her own hands. The two were united now. Well, let them perish together! When they left, she hoped it would be their last night on earth, that they would freeze before they reached home. And now, as she listened to the howling of the *buran*, her hate seemed stronger in her than her love.

Then she heard a different sound: groaning, snorting, and muffled knocking. Something dark appeared before the window and fell at the threshold. The girl seized a hatchet and went to the door.

"Who is there?" she asked, and receiving no answer, she boldly opened the door. Something big lay in the snow. She touched it with her foot and then with her hand. It was a horse. Uneasy and curious, she carefully examined the animal and recognized Antony's yellow mare.

Suddenly presented with this proof of disaster, she grew frightened, and her heart ached. She took care to ascertain that the animal was alive and covered it with a felt blanket. Then she stood for a moment, torn by conflicting thoughts.

Twice she approached Andryanek, only to draw back. The wind struck the walls of the house and howled. She remembered then that summer evening when the young scythe merchant stopped by for the first time. He spoke to her of her own country, and he taught her a song. He was a good man, very good.

She leaned against the wall and wept, and with her tears, her hatred floated away. She shook Andryanek awake.

"Get up! Antony's mare lies at the threshold."

"The mare's alone? Where are they?" muttered the sleepy peasant.

"They must have been buried in the snow!"

"What then?"

"Then go and search for them."

"Are you out of your mind? Is the steppe a market square that I could find them?"

"You stupid log! If the mare has found her way here, they cannot be far off. The horses were probably following their own tracks back to the *futor* until they lost their strength."

"Yes, but who will find the tracks now? It is you who are

being stupid!"

"My dogs will find them. Enough of this talk. The day breaks. Let us be going."

"You! Oh, my God!" muttered Andryanek. "Even if we find them, they are probably frozen to death!"

He and Lukovski got up.

The girl took three shovels, called the dogs, and, caressing them, let them smell a woolen scarf left by Antony some time ago, which she had kept in her trunk. Then she led the dogs into the yard, and let them smell the horses, then gave them the command:

"Search, search!"

The dogs went into the snow boldly, and the girl followed them with a shovel.

The wind was strong, and the snow filled their eyes. In order that they do not become separated, the girl tied a rope around her waist, and Andryanek and Lukovski held onto it. They advanced very slowly, for the dogs often lost the scent. They dug in the snow in a couple of places, turned around, and returned to the same place several times. The two men and the girl could barely walk, the snow was so deep.

After several hours of this hard work, they had only reached the birch grove, a few hundred steps from the house. The *futor* disappeared in the blizzard, and Andryanek said:

"May God help us find the house when night falls."

The girl struggled on, talking to the dogs all the while. All at once, both hounds rushed to a mound of snow and began to·dig with great ardor. The girl sank in the snow up to her knees and once fell into a snow drift up to her armpits, but she obstinately crawled on after the dogs.

"Oh, Lord!" muttered Andryanek to himself, "were I not married already, I would marry her. How strong she is!"

"The dogs have found something," shouted Lukovski.

"It must be the shaman, their master," answered the peasant.

192

Suddenly, he sank in the snow up to his neck and shouted:

"Holy God! Help! I have struck something hard."

Lukovski began to dig in the snow, and the wind blew the snow back in. It was hard work. The girl threw off her *tulub* and worked tirelessly. The struggle lasted about an hour, and they were growing tired. Finally, the shovel struck something hard: it was a horse's head, frozen stiff, with blood-flecked foam frozen on its mouth.

"It is them," whispered Andryanek. "They are already frozen."

Certainty gave them greater strength. They threw aside the snow with their hands and feet, the dogs worked with their noses. When they reached the furs and felts, something immediately moved underneath, and Tomoy jumped out, his whole body trembling. Zosha's dogs rushed at him, baring their fangs, but he would not stir from the furs, faithful to his mistress.

They tore away the frozen furs, and the girl seized Antony in her arms. He was stiff, white, and cold, like a piece of bone. He held a broken whip in one hand, his other arm was around his wife. The girl pulled him out and laid him on the snow. Andryanek lifted out Marya.

"They have suffocated," he said.

"No. They will live," muttered the girl.

"The place where the dog lay is warm," said Lukovski.

"That is true. Well, we must rub them and move them. Here is the vodka. Put some of it down their throats."

Having taken off their *tulubs*, they began to revive the unfortunate couple. Antony was the first to swallow some of the vodka. The girl rubbed him with snow and warmed him with her own breath.

"She is alive also!" shouted Andryanek. "Now we must carry them to the *futor* for warmth. The dogs will lead us."

He carried Marya, and the girl and Lukovski followed,

carrying Antony between them. Now the dogs did not hesitate, and the smoke of the house soon guided them.

The blizzard was still bewildering, and the way was difficult. They were minuscule particles moving in a great galaxy of swirling snow, and the steppe, furious for having been robbed of its prey, tried to blow them off its face. But that night, it did not accomplish its wish. In the house, under the influence of the warmth of the fire and the vodka, life returned to those two who had been buried alive. They awakened and looked at each other, then looked around.

"In the name of the Father and the Son!" exclaimed Antony, making a sign of the cross.

Marya saw Andryanek, the girl, and the fire and wept with happiness. Tomoy sat opposite her, looking into her eyes.

"My Lord!" said Antony in a whisper. "Have I dreamt it, or was I a dead man? It's a good thing to live!"

"You would not be alive any longer had it not been for the dogs," said the peasant. "And the girl. She saved you."

"God has been merciful to us. Where did you find us, and by what miracle?"

"Behind the birch grove. The dogs led us. You may well say it was a miracle. Now, mark my words. From now on, you will be successful in everything you do. If the *burun* has not killed you, then nothing can touch you. I am ready to go into partnership with you in any business you choose."

"It is not my luck. It is my wife's. If it were not for her, I should be a dead man today."

They were so weak that they could not stand.

Suddenly, the wind entered the house through the chimney, and the smoke from the fire filled the room. It was dark and cold and acrid.

"The devils are rejoicing over the shaman's death," said Andryanek.

Lukovski sat on the bench, looking at the girl. The dogs lay at her feet, and she was silent and gloomy again. Sometimes she looked from under her eyebrows at Mrozovetski. Finally, Andryanek began to talk about the steppe, with which he had been familiar from childhood. He had never seen a storm like this.

"A few winters ago, a whole wedding party was buried by a *burun*," he said indifferently. "Forty people and seven sleighs with horses were lost and could not be found. In the summer, someone discovered them by chance. The sleighs, people, and horses were standing in a row; the grass and weeds covered them, and there were plenty of birds' nests in the furs and felt. The hawks and foxes visited them; even the *tarbagans* were not afraid of them. In that way, the steppe gives life and death! Listen to how the blizzard howls. He is already tired, and pretty soon, he will lie down."

They all listened. Outside, the breathing of the wind could now only be heard from time to time. Then there came one more powerful roar, and—everything was quiet.

"Now the great frost will come," said the peasant. "He got bored with all this noise, and now he will give us silence. He is the lord of all."

And gradually, the steppe fell silent; the blizzard fell away, choked to death. A silvery light streamed through the window, and in a moment, the room became cold, and those inside shuddered. Outside there was great stillness, and the sky swarmed with millions of stars. The snow was quickly turning to stone, and suddenly the ice on the lake cracked with a loud thunder.

"This is your sign that the cold has won," said the peasant. "Had we deferred the rescue until now, you would not have lived."

"Well, we were fated to live. Such is our destiny," said Marya.

"And now you will be happy; you will see!"

Lukovski sat closer to the girl, whispering something to her. She seemed to pay no attention to him, but when, towards morning, they began to talk as to how they could get back without enough horses and sleighs, Lukovski said:

"You can all drive back in Andryanek's sleigh. I will remain here. I cannot leave my countrywoman alone."

The peasant looked at them and laughed.

"It's true," he affirmed.

At parting, Marya embraced the girl and whispered something in her ear, at which she blushed.

Then Antony said to her:

"Zosha, I judged you harshly. Forgive me. You have a good heart."

She looked at him.

"I loved you, Antony, and therefore·I wanted you to live," she muttered. "Because of me, you were unhappy; and now, because of me, you will be happy. Go, in God's name."

She turned away and began to play with the dogs. The bells resounded for a long time in the crystal clear, frosty air, and the sleigh floated smoothly over the snow like a boat over the silvery blue sea.

Andryanek whistled, and Marya said:

"Antony, this will be our last misadventure."

"And thanks be to God!"

THE END

OTHER GREAT BOOKS FROM OUR COLLECTION

From the same author:

A Summer of the Forest Folk
By Maria Rodziewiczówna

A classic feel-good story of friendship, coming of age, and the healing power of nature. Three women escape each summer to a remote cottage in the last virgin forest of Europe. This summer, they are joined by their big city nephew. Maria's greatest bestseller and a cult book for over 100 years. Find out why.
"Irresistibly charming!"

AND ALSO:

Seven Against Thebes
By Aleksander Krawczuk

Before the Trojan War, there was the Theban War. Greek heroes beneath the walls of Troy spoke with admiration about their fathers—the heroes the Theban War.
What was that war? Who fought it and why? What does archeology tell us? What have subsequent generations made of it?
"A classicist's escapist dream!"

Out of the Lion's Maw
By Witold Makowiecki

A European action-adventure bestseller set in the ancient Mediterranean. An elderly Zoroastrian priest and his young teen apprentice try to prevent the outbreak of a civil war in Egypt. Their opponent is the entire state apparatus of Eternal Egypt. Their resources: the old man's wit and the young man's courage. If you liked *The Three Musketeers* and *The Treasure Island*, you will like this.

"What a delightful and absorbing read!"

Out of the Lion's Maw
By Witold Makowiecki

In extraordinary times, twelve-year-old boys must act like men. Greece 562 BC. For insolvent debtors, the price of bankruptcy is slavery. When his mother and siblings are seized for unpaid debts, little Diossos must run to fetch help. He must cross mountains, forests, and stormy seas, brave wild animals, slave catchers, pirates, and police. He has a month to achieve his quest, only days to grow up. Plus...the hilarious heroes of *Out of the Lion's Maw* return for an encore.

"What an epic adventure!"

Divine Julius
By Jacek Bocheński

Would you like to become a god? It has been done, you know. A cynical look at the problem of how to coopt the elites and overturn the Republic. The book was published to great critical acclaim and almost immediately—banned: Polish authorities did not like how it laid bare the mechanism by which a tyranny manufactures consent. A modern classic, never out of print 60 years after its initial publication, and… a ripping read written in Caesar's own, telegraphic style.
"What a gift to have this in English!"

Naso the Poet
By Jacek Bocheński

Rome's greatest poet was sent into exile for life and his works were consigned to "damnatio memoriae": eternal forgetting.
But they weren't forgotten. Readers touched by their beauty have preserved their prized volumes and copied them by hand so that the literature which had offended their government may yet live on. And it has. But who was Ovid? And what crime did he commit to bring upon himself his punishment?
"It would be difficult to find a more brilliant fictional treatment of Ovid's life than this hilariously serious entertainment."
Theodore Ziolkowski, *Ovid and the Moderns"*